Cammy Takes A Bow

Avon Flare Books by
Karen Strickler Dean

BETWEEN DANCES:
Maggie Adams' Eighteenth Summer

MAGGIE ADAMS, DANCER

STAY ON YOUR TOES, MAGGIE ADAMS!

KAREN STRICKLER DEAN has been a balletomane for more than forty years. She studied with Bronislava and Irina Nijinska in Los Angeles and with the San Francisco Ballet School. In her novels for young readers, she hopes to convey the excitement of ballet while showing a realistic portrait of a dancer's world.

KAREN STRICKLER DEAN has been writing since she was nine years old and has written six published books and a number of articles and short stories for magazines and educational publications. Formerly a school teacher for children with learning disabilities, she lives in Palo Alto, California, with her husband. They have four grown children.

Cammy Takes A Bow

Karen Strickler Dean

AN AVON CAMELOT BOOK

AVON BOOKS
A division of
The Hearst Corporation
105 Madison Avenue
New York, New York 10016

Dedicated to the memory of my father,
R.V. Strickler,
who painted first surrounded by his children,
later by his grandchildren

Acknowledgments

Special thanks for reading this book in manuscript and for making thoughtful suggestions go to Robyn Crumly, watercolor artist, and to Laura Van Dilla, of the National Sibling Network (5112 15th Avenue South, Minneapolis, MN 55417), an organization for the siblings and children of the mentally ill.

Chapter One

A Class Audition

Today's ballet lesson was the most important in my whole, entire life. It wasn't just any old class. It was an audition for the children's parts in Blikk Eriksen's new ballet, *Beauty and the Beast*.

"Concentrate, Cammy," our teacher Madame Harper called from her chair at the front of the classroom. "Raising your hip, darling child, is not the correct way to shift from first to second position. It makes your leg only seem to go higher. And it won't impress Mr. Eriksen."

My face blazed, must have turned as red as my hair. Vermilion, the color Daddy uses in watercolor sketches of me and my creepy brother Luke.

I mean, Blikk Eriksen not only directs the ballet school, he directs the entire City Ballet Association of San Francisco and choreographs most of its ballets. He's in complete, total charge of everything, including casting.

My braid, thick and slippery as rope, pulled free of all the bobby pins I had jammed in before class and skidded down from its topknot. Chewing the frizzy tip, I tightened my rear end and pushed my leg around to the back.

Blikk Eriksen just had to choose me. The kids he picked,

1

especially if they also did well in the school's end of the year demonstration program, were sure to get scholarships. Which were really scarce. But without one paying at least half my tuition again next year—particularly with only Mom working these days—I'd have to stop taking ballet. Then how would I ever become a dancer like Maggie Adams?

Madame Harper's metal chair squawked. Behind her, the wall of mirrors reflected her slim back in black leotard and full, gauzy skirt. A snowy part split her shiny, dark head into two equal halves. Her long earrings swung, chimed, and glinted with highlights. "Cammy darling, watch Madelaine. She keeps her hip down beautifully."

"Yes, Madame," I said, clenching my mouth until my braces bit into the undersides of my lips. Down the *barre* from me Madelaine balanced on a leg thin as a soda straw. The other stretched high, nudging the hay-colored split ends unraveling from her topknot. She was new here. Only started taking class two months ago when the ballet school reopened after the holidays.

None of us knew a thing about her except that she was nearly thirteen, almost two years older than the rest of us. She hardly ever talked. Of course, I had been a little shy, too, when I first came here a year and a half ago. But, from the beginning, I at least used to grin and say, "Hi," instead of just curling my lips into a smile as limp as wet tights like this Madelaine did.

Also, she never changed clothes in our packed dressing room that stank of sweat and Johnson's Baby Powder. She was delivered in a white Mercedes, all ready for class and trailing some flowery scent. And the Mercedes was driven, not by her mom, but by a sharp-nosed chauffeur. He whisked her away afterwards, too.

So it was really obvious that Madelaine didn't need a scholarship. It was equally obvious, however, that she was trying for one. Why else at the start of every class did she skitter to the spot at the *barre* directly opposite the only

2

mirror that didn't reflect you either fat as a pumpkin or skinny as a string bean? Later, why did she always scurry to the exact center of the front row for floor exercises? To draw attention to herself, that was why. And at today's audition she was the only student who, to be noticed no doubt, had tied a ribbon around her topknot. A red ribbon. Vermilion.

Again her pipe-cleaner leg floated high to the side. Her instep positively kissed her ear.

I thrust out my chin. If Madelaine's foot could touch her ear, so could mine! I tensed my rear end, thrust my working leg forward, then hoisted it around into a high second position.

"Hip down, Cammy," Madame Harper said, her earrings clinking. "And the rest of you, my darlings, are raising your hips, too."

Our teacher struggled out of her chair and lurched across the room. Tendonitis in her Achilles tendons had forced her to retire as the company's prima ballerina a few months ago. Now she taught us, second year students in the school's professional division.

"Darlings, come watch Madelaine."

"Madelaine. Always Madelaine," I grumbled to Helen, who was working next to me at the *barre*. "What's so great about kicking your own ear?"

"Madelaine's just a paragon, that's all," said Helen. Helen's a regular walking dictionary, always reading. Which might be how she got so nearsighted that she had to wear those thick, round glasses. "A paragon's someone who's a good example of something, you know," she added, wriggling her thick, caterpillar eyebrows at me.

I lifted my chin. "I know what a paragon is."

One corner of Helen's mouth tucked into its half-grin. "Now you know!"

"Helen and Cammy," Madame called, "I said, come watch Madelaine."

"Yes, Madame." Then I muttered to Helen, "What Madelaine is a paragon at is getting noticed while pretending

3

she couldn't care less about Blikk Eriksen's ballet or the demonstration or a scholarship. Look at her. Except for the red ribbon, she's cool as the doll Mom gave me last month for my birthday. An old fashioned Bye-lo Baby doll.''

"A baby doll when you turned eleven?" Helen whispered, squinting anxiously through her glasses at Madame. "Good grief!"

I shrugged. "It's not to play with, dummy. That's why I didn't get it till I was eleven, old enough not to smash it. The head's made of porcelain. The Bye-lo belonged to my great-grandmother, the one named Cameo, the same as me. Only they actually called her Cameo. Ugh!"

"Too much!" Helen said, with a side glance at Madame Harper.

I nodded. "You said it. And Cameo's daughter, my grandmother, got the doll when she was eleven and my mother when she was eleven."

"And you when you were eleven," Helen finished for me.

I grinned. "Yeah. Whether I wanted it or not."

Which I hadn't, never having gone in for dolls even before I started ballet. Then, if I wasn't booting a soccer ball or getting blisters from parallel bars, I'd be scrambling between our eaves and the giant oak tree. Right behind me would come my brother Luke, red hair flying, bellowing Tarzan yells. That was his Tarzan stage. He wanted to star in Tarzan movies.

Luke was three years younger than I but we used to get along okay. Used to. No more. Now all the brat did was tease me, leaping around, imitating my dancing. He also stuck up yellow, sticky-backed Post-it Notes swiped from Mom's desk and proclaiming embarrassing information about me. Like the one a couple of weeks ago when I was barely over the stomach flu. Planted on the upstairs hall rug and correctly spelled for a change, it said, "Cammy Smith puked here."

4

"The Bye-lo doll isn't even pretty," I continued to Helen. "Its head is bald as a light bulb."

"Shush, Cam, Madame's glaring at us again," Helen whispered, trying not to wheeze. Among other things, she was allergic to acacias, whose fuzzy yellow balls were blooming everywhere now that spring had begun.

"Stop the talking," our teacher snapped, "and come watch Madelaine."

"Rats," I grumbled.

"Ditto," Helen said.

But we tromped closer to Madelaine, whose stick-thin leg repeated its ear-kissing miracle.

"It practically levitates," Helen whispered. "Sort of drifts up, you know, Cam."

I clenched my lips over my braces. "I know."

I also knew that I was not as limber as Madelaine and that my leg would never levitate like hers. I sighed.

But so what? I flipped my braid over my shoulder and tilted my chin. Weren't my little jumps and sliding *glissades* just as light and quick as before she came?

"Know what, Helen?" We two were the only ones not hovering close to Madelaine, breathing in her flowery cologne. "Helen, I've made up my mind. Blikk Eriksen is positively going to adore my dancing. He'll think it's the greatest."

Helen wiggled her eyebrows above the rims of her glasses. "Oh, yeah?"

"Yeah. Listen, Helen, when he gets here my extensions will nudge one of the fluorescent ceiling lamps. They'll soar so sky-high that he'll stare in pure astonishment. He'll whisper to Madame Harper: 'Why, my dear Natalie, who is that talented, auburn-haired beauty with the incredible beats and amazing extensions?' "

Helen's mouth folded into its half-grin. "Carrot-red, you mean. About beauty, I don't know. More like pointy-chinned

5

and pixieish. And, Cam, be careful you don't pull a tendon or something."

I grinned. "Not me."

"Buzz, buzz, buzz," Madame hissed. "Cammy and Helen, I asked you to watch Madelaine."

"Sorry, Madame." Followed by Helen, I scuffed two steps closer.

"And then Madame'll say," I continued in a low voice to Helen, "Madame'll say, 'Why, darling, you remember darling Cammy Smith. She danced in *Nutcracker* last December. Cammy's a true paragon. Did you ever see such levitating leaps and extravagant extensions?' And he'll say, 'My dear Natalie, I really must have this gifted student in my *Beauty and the Beast.*' "

"Dreamer!" Helen said, her eyebrows wobbling like a pair of drunk caterpillars. "And I suppose he'll give you the role of Beauty's Little Sister."

"Sure. Why not? Maggie Adams is dancing Beauty and we're both redheads, aren't we? And sisters usually have hair the same color."

"Cammy and Helen, pay attention," Madame Harper barked. "I don't want to have to speak to you again. You could both learn a great deal from Madelaine."

"Yes, Madame," I muttered.

"Yes, Madame," Helen echoed.

Like magic, up wafted Madelaine's leg again. And, wouldn't you know, at that very moment the door latch clicked behind us. I caught my breath. Blikk Eriksen!

My heart fluttered against my ribs. But I didn't dare look around at him.

Madelaine dared, though. Her cheeks reddened to match the ribbon in her hair. Her blue eyes widened, practically clicking in the silence like the Bye-lo's when they opened or shut. And the Paragon's skinny leg floated higher than ever before.

6

I let out my breath. So did the rest of the students, including Madelaine. The studio filled with one long sigh.

Only then did I glance at Blikk Eriksen. Lean and shorter than Daddy, he bobbed into the room like the dancer he used to be.

I licked my braces. Blikk Eriksen just had to like my dancing. My whole life depended on it.

Chapter Two

The Blue Streaker

Into the classroom with Blikk Eriksen came Maggie Adams, my very favorite dancer, teetering in high-heeled red pumps. She flipped back her long, bright hair. It was curly, not slick and straight like mine. Wouldn't Daddy love to paint hers— all crinkly and full of light!

"Good afternoon, ladies," Blikk Eriksen said, shifting from one hand to the other the thick notebook he always carried to make notes in about his ballets. He smiled around at everybody.

Helen sighed. "Oh, swoon!"

Several kids giggled nervously, including me. Madelaine may have giggled, too, but I doubted it. All I knew for sure was that every time I looked at her, she was weaving her fingers together and looking at me.

"What's her problem?" I whispered to Helen.

"She's worried about her main competition, silly. You're it."

"Me? Do you really think so?"

But Helen shushed me because Madame Harper was eyeing us and Blikk Eriksen was talking.

"Maggie and I are here to become better acquainted with

8

all of you," he said. "Also, as you know, to select students to perform in *Beauty and the Beast*. It will be danced as the season opener and then not again until late spring. So rehearsing for it will not interfere with rehearsals for your demonstration, *Window on the Future*. And since Maggie will be dancing Beauty she wants to help me choose the girl for the role of Beauty's Little Sister."

Helen poked me. "You, Cam, you!"

I ducked my head. "Stop it, Helen!"

She nudged me again. "Look at the Paragon. She's dying for the role, same as you, Cam. Check her out."

Helen was right. Madelaine's cheeks blazed. Her blue eyes glinted. Her gaze jumped from grown-up to grown-up. And, under the black leotard required by the school dress code, her narrow chest panted in and out, in and out, as if she had just finished one of Madame Harper's *grand jeté* combinations.

Our teacher limped to the center of the room to welcome Blikk Eriksen and Maggie.

"My students are a little tense this afternoon," Madame said, laughing and swinging her earrings as if this was just an ordinary class and not a really important audition. I chewed the frayed tip of my braid.

"They don't know quite what to expect, being only second year students. Except Madelaine over there at the middle of the *barre*. She's had a bit more training as well as some stage experience in New York. You'll remember, Blikk darling, we decided to put her here in Class Two because her feet sickled in a little. She also needed to work on her turn-out and pick up some basics that she had missed in the East. Besides, she hadn't taken class for almost a year."

"New York, huh!" I muttered to Helen. "More training, too! Then she's a shoo-in for Beauty's Little Sister. Not to mention the front row, center spot in the dance our class is working on for the demonstration. Those'll add up to one huge scholarship."

9

"Which she needs about as much as the Queen of England," Helen said.

"Yeah. About as much," I said, sighing. Then, frowning, I asked, "Why do you suppose she didn't take class for a whole year?"

Helen only shrugged and Madame was saying, "I'm wondering, Blikk, would you care to teach the rest of the class?"

My heart leaped. "He can't!" I moaned to Helen.

"That way, darling, you could give the kinds of steps you'll expect them to do in your ballet."

I nibbled the tip of my braid. If Blikk Eriksen took over, no telling what utterly hopeless steps he'd give us. Double *pirouettes*. Feet flickering *entrechats-quatre*. Things we'd never, ever had before. Except maybe the New York Paragon, even if she hadn't taken class for a year. And doing those steps would really make her stand out, even without the red ribbon.

"Advise me, Maggie," Blikk Eriksen was saying, his gray eyes bright with highlights. "Should I or should I not take over Madame Harper's delightful class?"

"Oh, please, no!" I blurted. I hadn't meant to. The words just popped out.

Blikk Eriksen's eyes crinkled above the smile he sent me. "I think the nays have it, judging by Cammy's reaction and all the white, anxious faces I see around me. And I do believe your students will be more relaxed if you continue, Natalie."

He always talked as if he were reading from a book. He grew up in Norway, an article in *Dance Magazine* said, and only learned English later when he was studying ballet in London.

The three grown-ups dropped onto metal chairs in front of the mirrors. Squawk. Squawk. Squawk. I shuddered at the harsh sounds and hoped our teacher wouldn't ask for *développés* again. Touching her red ribbon, Madelaine probably hoped Madame would.

But she didn't. Madame Harper skipped to *pirouettes*, then finished *barre* work with *grands battements*, a cinch for me.

After she called us to the center for floor exercises, though, she did want *développés* again.

"And hips down, darling children, particularly in second position," Madame said but at least she didn't single me out and say, "That means you, Cammy Smith!" If she had in front of Maggie Adams and Blikk Eriksen, I'd have died! What Madame did do, though, was ask the New York Paragon to demonstrate the combination. I hunched my shoulders. Madelaine and her red ribbon!

"Without the piano, Madelaine," Madame Harper added. "I want to make sure that everyone knows how to count the combination."

I clamped my mouth over my braces. The thin wire fences made my teeth ache.

And, glancing at me over her bony shoulder, Madelaine wedged her feet into a tight fifth position. She *pliéd*, and, looking as thin as a pipe-cleaner doll, slid forward to fourth. Closing to fifth again, she began the *développé*. She arched her right foot in its immaculate rose-bud pink slipper, drew it up her left leg, then slowly, slowly unfolded her working leg toward the mirror.

I licked my braces. Oh please, let her make a mistake. Let her raise her hip or jerk her leg when it passes from first to second position. Let her foot sickle in like it used to.

But her foot didn't sickle, her hip didn't lift, and her leg didn't jerk. She moved slowly, evenly.

"Very nice," Madame Harper said. "Now ease your leg to the rear. Lovely, my darling," the teacher added when Madelaine had finished and was retying her red ribbon. "Does everyone know the combination now?"

"Of course, we know the steps," I grumbled just loud enough for Helen to hear. "We're not morons."

Sighing, Helen squinted through her glasses. Poor Helen can't wear contact lenses because allergies make her eyes

11

too sensitive. "Maybe some of us are morons," she said. "At least as far as dancing is concerned. Me, for instance."

"Oh, come on, Helen, you do okay," I said, not looking at her because lots of times she didn't. How she passed the audition to get into the professional division or survived the end of the year exams to stay in, I'd never know.

I shifted my feet to the starting position. The music began and, running my tongue over my braces, I concentrated on turning out, on keeping my hip down, but especially on pushing my leg really high. Suddenly, though, something in my left thigh snapped. I gave a grunt but kept on working. Still warm from *barre* work, I didn't have much pain.

I just hoped my rubbery face, that Mom claimed showed all my thoughts and feelings, hadn't revealed my pain. No way would Blikk Eriksen cast his new ballet with people who injured themselves every two seconds.

"Good, Cammy," Madame Harper said when we had finished the combination.

Happiness leaped like a deer inside me. Had Blikk Eriksen and Maggie noticed how well I had danced, too? But they were bending over his thick notebook.

"Now *pirouettes* from fourth position," Madame Harper called. "Singles, please. Show us, Madelaine."

"Oh, not again," I mumbled to Helen.

"It must be the red ribbon," she said.

Alone in the center of the room the Paragon stopped twisting her fingers and slid her feet into fourth position. She demonstrated a *pirouette* so slow, so perfectly balanced, that even I gasped. At the end of it, she hovered on the ball of one foot for a breath-taking couple of seconds before settling into fifth position. At first only silence. Then applause. At the front of the room Blikk Eriksen and Maggie buzzed together. A tiny smile lifted the corners of Madelaine's mouth.

I licked my braces. Goodbye to the role I wanted. And the scholarship.

"Thank you, Madelaine darling," Madame Harper said.

12

"Now the rest of you. Remember, your center of balance is in your waist. So pull up. Pull up." She raised an eyebrow at me because sometimes I fall off my *pirouettes*. She nodded to the pianist to begin playing.

I pulled up in spite of my aching thigh and managed the first *pirouette*. Then, even with my leg hurting and my soggy braid hitting me in the mouth, I spun the second.

"Very nice, Cammy," the teacher called. And she actually asked me to demonstrate the next combination. Little jumps! What I did best. When I wasn't injured, that is. Excitement shivered through me. Maybe I'd win the part I wanted in *Beauty*, after all. Maybe a first row spot in *Window*, too. And receive a whole scholarship next year.

If only my hurt leg didn't spoil my dancing.

Madame Harper signaled for music. And to a lilting Chopin melody, my feet skimmed along the floor, soared into a pair of *jetés*, then lifted in *changements*. I repeated the combination in the opposite direction, noticing no pain. Then I waited, breathing hard.

Would everyone clap for me as they had for Madelaine?

But titters flooded the room. Even Helen, my best friend, was giggling. Madelaine smiled, showing two rows of even, braceless teeth, and began clapping. Also applauding were Blikk Eriksen, Maggie Adams, and Madame Harper. Absolutely everybody. And a glance at the mirror showed me that the clapping wasn't for me.

In it colors flashed and blended. A streak of blue jeans. A blur of blue turtle neck. A smudge of blue and white running shoes. Pumping blue legs. Longish red hair leaping like flames. One joyful jump after another. And a big smirk. They were clapping for my brother Luke.

13

Chapter Three

A Wild Trip Home

As soon as I recognized Luke, I took off. I didn't wait for class to finish or for the results of the audition. I left as fast as I could on my hurt leg.

But not before girls swarmed around him, giggling and cooing. "Adorable." "So cute." Even Madelaine, her straw-colored permanent towering above the heads of the others, smiled at him from the sidelines of the crowd.

Downstairs in the dressing room I yanked jeans and sweater on top of my sweaty practice clothes. Then, slinging my satchel over my shoulder, I headed toward the foyer. Mom would be waiting on one of the plastic-covered sofas, drained after a day of trying to figure out why certain kids at her school were so off-the-wall that they couldn't learn.

I set my feet down carefully to keep from limping. I didn't grab an ice pack from the physical therapy room. If Mom found out I'd hurt myself she might claim I was injury prone and add that to her reasons for me to quit ballet. Number one was her dumb idea that I didn't have enough talent.

But Mom wasn't waiting in the foyer with the rest of the mothers, including Helen's, who worked as a secretary somewhere.

At the front door, though, we collided as Mom dashed in and I hobbled out.

"Mom, how come you let Luke go upstairs?"

"Let him? I told him to wait here while I brought the station wagon around. I've got the engine running out front. I was afraid the heap would die if I turned it off. Exactly where is he now?"

"Well, he didn't wait. Oh, Mom, he was such a brat. Why can't you ever get him to do what you say? Isn't a school psychologist like you supposed to get kids to mind?"

"I do the best I can, my girl! But today with the schools in your district closed for teacher study sessions or some such nonsense and your father off peddling watercolors to the galleries, Luke was cooped up in my office all day. He had to let a little steam off somehow."

"Steam! But not by bursting into my class! Jumping all over the place. Making everybody laugh. I could have died!"

Behind us Luke's high, bubbling voice whooped down the stairs. "Another Baryshnikov. That's what they all called me! Another Baryshnikov, like that terrific dancer on TV."

Despite my hurt leg, I spun to face my brother. Grinning, he bounced toward us across the foyer. His hair blew in red streamers above his head. If the kids in my class thought he was adorable, it had to be because they didn't live with him or go to the same school with him. Now he had even invaded my ballet class!

"Hey, Mom, guess what?" he said. "I'm a fabulous jumper. Sensational! Really talented. That's what everybody said. All those girls. Especially the tall one. The pretty one, Madelaine."

I sniffed. "That dishrag! What does she know?"

Luke stuck out his lower lip. "A lot. And the man thought I was fantastic, too."

I scowled. "What man? Who are you talking about?"

Grinning, Luke made owl eyes at me but ignored my question. "Mom, the man asked where I'd learned to jump. I

15

said I didn't learn. I just jump. So he claimed I'm a natural and then I told him about winning the contest.''

I tossed back my braid. ''What contest? What are you talking about?''

''The Super-Duper, Worldwide Easter Bunny Jumping Contest. Don't you even remember? I jumped higher than any kid in class.''

''That was three years ago. That was when you were still in kindergarten.''

Luke frowned. For an instant his mouth sagged and grew soft. The freckles splotched across his nose and cheeks darkened. Then he flipped the bang of red hair off his forehead. ''So what? I won, didn't I? The man upstairs called me another Baryshnikov because I jumped higher than anybody in your class. Including, you, Cameo Cammy,'' he said. His teasing grin quirked up one corner of his mouth and made his eyes shine as green as two traffic lights signaling ''go.''

I made a grab for him but he dodged. ''What man are you talking about?'' I yelled again. As if I didn't know!

Mom rubbed her temples. ''Be quiet, both of you. Today's only Wednesday, but it seemed like Friday with Luke under foot every second, plus my usual explosive crew! I can't take much more.''

Luke glanced at Mom, then away and made owl eyes at me again. ''The only man there, dummy. The guy with the gray hair. The one with the silvery eyes. The one clapping for me and laughing his head off.''

I gripped my hands so hard that my fingernails bit into my palms. ''Blikk Eriksen! You've ruined my whole, entire life, you little creep. Mom, you've got to do something about Luke!''

But Mom went on massaging her temples.

''It's just not fair,'' I sputtered and, forgetting my injury, whirled toward the front door. I groaned with pain and hobbled the rest of the way out to the sidewalk.

At the curb, in a red, no-parking zone, rumbled Old

16

Faithful, our banged-up station wagon. Its crumpled headlight resulted from Mom tangling with the power pole at one side of our driveway. A spattering of yellow acacia puffs danced on its shuddering hood.

Yanking open the back door, I flung myself onto the rear seat. I let out a yowl of pain. But when Mom came out of the studio, I stopped clutching my hurt leg.

She sagged into the driver's seat. Luke scrambled in beside her and after a peek at her face, grinned over his shoulder at me. Facing around, he bounced up and down as if his rear end consisted entirely of foam rubber.

"Yay. Yay, I jumped clear to the ceiling! A hundred times higher than you, Cammy Wammy!"

"Mother! Make Luke shut up!"

"Sit," she ordered him and, stiffening her index finger, pointed at the seat. "Fasten your seatbelts, both of you." By her crankiness and the way her fingers pressed her forehead, I knew she had one of her Friday headaches although it was only Wednesday. "I want complete, absolute silence all the way home. I am not up to dealing with any more hyperactive juveniles today."

I sighed. It had been bad enough when she was writing her Master's thesis and studying for her comprehensive exams. But since getting this job as a school psychologist last September, she'd been crabbier than ever.

She turned the key in the ignition but the motor gave only a metallic squawk. She tried again. Same thing. "Ridiculous thing's flooded," she said.

Madelaine's white Mercedes flowed up to us and double parked alongside. Opening his door, the chauffeur stuck his long nose above the car's shiny white roof and peered toward the ballet school.

"What a beauty!" Luke said. "That's what we need, Mom, a Mercedes with a chauffeur with a green cap and uniform."

"That'll be the day," Mom growled, "with your father

17

home painting dozens of unsaleable watercolors and only me working."

"Look who's getting into that beauty," Luke yelped. "The beauty named Madelaine! Man, her father must be a billionaire!" And rolling down his window, Luke poked his head through the opening. "Hey, Madelaine."

My face burning, I ducked down on the back seat. "Honestly, Luke! She doesn't even know who you are."

But she turned, her pale eyes wide as sand dollars on the beach where Daddy paints sometimes. A faint smile turned up the corners of her mouth. Waving just the tips of her fingers, she called softly, "Bye, bye, Luke."

I felt like puking.

"Doesn't know who I am, does she?" Luke crowed, sticking out his tongue at me. Just as our engine coughed and started, he bellowed, "See ya, Madelaine."

"Shut that window!" Mom barked and cut the station wagon in front of Madelaine's double-parked Mercedes and into the line of traffic. Horns blared. Brakes squawked. Madelaine's chauffeur thrust his head out his lowered window. "Watch it, lady!"

Mom thumbed her nose at him. I could have died!

Luke exploded with laughter, got up on his knees, thumbed his nose, too, then waved at Madelaine.

"Sit!" Mom snapped. She took one hand off the wheel to point her finger at the seat. She wheeled in front of a Porsche and zipped around an orange Volkswagen. More horns and slammed brakes!

I slumped lower on the rear seat. "For gosh sakes, Mom, are you trying to kill us or something? I can't stand the way you drive!"

"Well, you may not have to much longer," Mom said. "Remember, unless you win a full-tuition scholarship, that's the end of your dancing lessons. We just can't afford them."

I caught my breath but she went right on. "And I wouldn't exactly miss bucking San Francisco's cross-town traffic at 5

P.M. to pick you up from ballet. Come fall, it would be six days, not just three. And, for the sake of my sanity, Cammy, stop chewing your braid."

Unhooking my seatbelt, I grabbed the back of the driver's seat. "But, Mom, Mom, if you hate picking me up so much, I could ride the train home like I take it up here."

"You'll do no such thing. Not at your age. An eleven-year-old's too young to be traipsing through San Francisco and down the peninsula after dark. And how would you get home from the depot, I'd like to know?"

I stuck out my lower lip. "What's wrong with the bus?"

Mom sighed. "There's no point in going on about this, Cammy. Transportation isn't the real problem, it's the money. If the school doesn't think you're talented enough for a full scholarship next year, no ballet. End of discussion."

I let out a yowl. Luke widened his eyes at me. And, Mom, spinning right on a red light, shot into an opening in the parkway traffic hardly long enough for a skateboard. Another chorus of horns and brakes.

Luke chortled. "Right on, Mom!"

I slid back and refastened my seatbelt. After things had calmed down a little, I said as politely as I could, "But, Mom, I've just got to be a dancer."

"Got to? Got to? Cammy, you have to face reality now, rather than after years and years of expensive lessons. Ballet's very competitive. Requires real talent."

"I've got real talent. How else could I have passed the audition to get into the professional division?"

Mom shook her head. "I don't know, Honey. I hope you're right; I know how much it means to you. And I know your father believes you're talented. But of course he has lots more time than I have these days to think about such things, staying home trying to develop some God-given gifts of his own."

19

Chapter Four

Lukenikov

I was out the rear door as soon as Old Faithful bounded onto the driveway. Luke's fox terrier came leaping and yipping across the weeds and asphalt. "Down, Foxy! Stay down!"

Trying not to limp, I waded carefully through the shaggy lawn. The wooden steps and front porch groaned under my feet. Like lots of things in and out of our sprawling, old house, they needed fixing. Mom thought Daddy should do all the repairs. He said that wasn't their bargain. They only agreed that after putting her through graduate school, he got to take a year off, not to be a handyman, but to be a full-time artist.

I yanked open the screen door. Its hinges whined.

Bursting into the living room, I wailed, "Oh, Daddy, Daddy, you've just got to help me."

Daddy glanced up from his painting table. His wide mouth curled into a grin. He waved a watercolor brush at me.

"Hi, Honey Bunch. I'll be with you in a sec. I'm in the middle of a wash." He hunched over his table again, humming *Happy Days Are Here Again*.

A few minutes later he straightened his back. "There. Now I can let it dry. What's the problem, Poody Squash?

Not another utterly hopeless ballet class, I hope, I hope, I hope."

Grinning, he angled both elbows above his head. He was imitating ballet's fifth position *port de bras*, but he looked more like a sugar bowl.

"Oh, Daddy, don't tease me," I wailed, flinging myself across the living room and into his arms. My face pressed into the smelly, itchy wool of his paint-smeared gray sweater.

"Today was utterly hopeless, Daddy. First, that new girl Madelaine turns out to be from New York and will probably get all the good roles. Then Luke completely ruins the audition for me. And then Mom says that if I don't get a full-tuition scholarship next year I can't take ballet ever again. So how can I possibly be a dancer? Which I want to be more than anything in the whole, entire world. I'll just die."

He hugged and patted me. Then, easing me away a little, he balanced his brush across the rim of the mason jar he'd been using to rinse his brushes. The cloudy, yellowy-green water and the Thalo green stains on his fingertips meant he'd been painting the bay or the ocean.

Taped to his board lay a sheet of rough paper washed with greens and yellows. Waves shone in the sunlight and skimmed, lace-edged, onto a burnt sienna beach. Lots of times he painted Mom, me, or Luke. He said he liked our bright hair and pale skin. So I bet he'd adore Maggie's.

Daddy tightened his arms around me again. "Now, Honey Bunch, things can't be as bad as you think."

He hummed *Happy Days* until Foxy and Luke hurled themselves into the room. Luke's blue and white running shoes smacked the hardwood floor. Foxy's toenails clacked it.

"Hey, Dad," Luke shouted above Foxy's yapping. "Know what I did today, Dad? I jumped way higher than Cammy, higher than the moon. And I met Madelaine, this really neat girl in Cammy's ballet class."

21

I sniffed. "Stuck-up's more like it. Besides her feet sickle," I said, though, of course, they didn't much anymore except when she was tired. Depend on my brother to latch onto the one girl in my class I can't stand!

"Wanna see me jump, Dad?" Luke asked.

He didn't wait for an answer. When did he? Knees stiff, back arched, he jumped and jumped. Foxy leaped too, yipping ecstatically. His stump of a tail quivered.

"Good for you, Luke," Daddy said. "Now why don't you quietly take Foxy out to the kitchen and quietly feed him his dinner? And while you're at it, quietly feed yourself a peanut butter sandwich. That should hold you till Mom manages to get dinner on the table."

"Good thinking, Dad," Luke said with a smirk at me.

He and Foxy scuffed out to the kitchen just as Mom banged in at the front door. A grocery sack overflowing with celery tops and French bread crackled under each arm. As usual she had stopped at the Marina Safeway before picking me up from ballet.

"What was that all about, Lloyd?" Mom demanded to know. " 'Until Mom manages to get dinner on the table.' If you tossed the potatoes in the oven as I asked and scraped a few carrots, dinner should be about ready. Or would going to the kitchen for two seconds have ruined a priceless watercolor wash?"

I ducked my head and shrank against the bookcase wall. After working with those wild kids all day, Mom got pretty touchy. It was a good idea to stay out of her way at least until after dinner.

Daddy ran a hand through his soft, sand-colored hair and over the pink bald spot at the crown of his head. "The carrots are ready for steaming, Alice. The potatoes are baking. Take a whiff."

I smelled them now and Mom sighed. "Sorry. Just another rotten day in paradise. And having Luke underfoot didn't help any."

Daddy grinned. "I know. That's why I sent him out to the kitchen. Sorry he couldn't stay with me but I had the appointment at that gallery in Palo Alto."

"Did anything come of it?" Mom asked.

Daddy shrugged. "The man said he's swamped with seascapes."

"Then maybe you should try painting something more saleable."

"Yeah, Daddy. How about ballet?" I asked.

Mom groaned. "Ballet, ballet, ballet! She's obsessed with it, Lloyd. Eats, sleeps, and breathes ballet. Like you and your painting. And it's just about as practical."

I hunched my shoulders. Now she'd start about how we didn't have enough talent, Daddy and I.

But she staggered with the grocery sacks and muttered, "You might help me with these, Lloyd." Her legs buckled. Daddy grabbed the bags just before she toppled backward onto the sofa.

"Not there," he yelled. Too late. Mom crunched onto one of the half dozen crisp watercolors spread out to dry.

Mom leaped up. "Oh, I'm sorry, Lloyd. I didn't see them. Honestly, I didn't. But they're scattered everywhere." Her fingers pressed her forehead. She pivoted in her low-heeled brown loafers. "Like laundry, Lloyd. Like diapers drying. I didn't ruin it, did I?"

Daddy settled the grocery sacks on the floor and lifted the crumpled painting on his palms like a jeweled crown or something. Grinning, he pointed to the upper part of the sheet. "Not too bad, is it? Nice, clear color. Translucent. Center's muddy, though. So don't worry, Alice, it's no great loss." He crushed the paper into a ball and pitched it overhand and backward toward a waste basket. The wad missed and joined a dozen others on the floor.

"You might at least pick them up," Mom said, rubbing her temples. "This room's a disaster. And couldn't you use the backs of the sheets for other paintings, Lloyd? Watercolor paper costs a fortune these days." Her voice was growing shriller as she spoke.

Daddy lifted his shoulders slightly. Turning away, he frowned down at the painting drying on his work table. He poked at the colors to make sure they were no longer wet. "Fair to middling," he commented.

"Can't you forget your infernal painting for two seconds?" Mom asked. "A beginning psychologist's salary is a lot less than yours was as an engineer. We've got to cut down on expenses. Like on watercolor paper. Like on ballet lessons, too. Because studying ballet without enough talent is a waste of time and money."

"But Mom," I howled, "the people at the school thought I was talented enough for a scholarship this year."

She eyed me. "Half a scholarship. But what about next year?"

I licked my braces. "Well, if Luke hadn't come barging into the middle of the audition . . ."

"Blaming Luke doesn't change the situation. Cammy, you just have to face the possibility that you won't be able to continue ballet. I don't want you to be crushed if you don't get a scholarship for next year."

"But I *have* to, Mom!"

"Everybody just calm down," Daddy said, stripping off the tape that secured a painting to his drawing board. "And stop worrying about money, Alice. Unless I really succeed at painting, I'll probably go back to engineering after my year's leave of absence is up. In the meantime, we have savings. You'll get a raise."

"But will we have enough for everything, Lloyd? Mortgage payments? Braces for Luke?"

I thrust my chin forward. "And ballet lessons for me."

Daddy grinned. "We'll try to manage even that, Poody Squash. Who knows, a miracle might happen. I might sell a painting."

He hugged Mom and me against his scratchy old sweater.

24

"Hey, when's dinner?" Luke yelled, hurtling into the room. Foxy yipped around his knees. Suddenly, sideways to the floor, his hand clutching a peanut butter sandwich, Luke threw himself into the air, hovered, spun like a pastry whip beating eggs, and crash-landed.

I gasped. Now, where had he learned to do that? I didn't even know what to call it—if his whirling leap had a name.

"How'd you like it?" Luke shouted, springing to his feet. "Baryshnikov did that on TV. Except his landing wasn't quite as loud and spectacular. And, Mom, Dad," my brother added, snatching his sandwich out of Foxy's reach, "I've decided all those people at Cam's ballet school are absolutely right. Including that Madelaine girl. I am a natural jumper. So I'm going to become another Baryshnikov."

Mom and I stared. Daddy grinned. "I thought you were going to become another soccer star like Pélé."

"That was last month," Luke said. "Do you think I should call myself Luke Baryshnikov or just plain Lukenikov?"

Chapter Five

Lukenikov's Sister

Daddy sent Mom up to rest while he finished fixing supper. I went upstairs, too, to soak in the tub. I filled it to the top although Mom's always harping about not wasting hot water. But I figured that I needed gallons and gallons to help my leg and to help me forget the Paragon. She would probably get a good part in *Beauty* and, although only the advanced classes had soloists in the *Window on the Future* demonstration, she'd probably get the front row, center spot and wind up with a super big scholarship. Which I needed, not Madelaine.

I was up to my neck in hot water when Luke banged on the bathroom door. He never knocks like an ordinary person.

From the hall he bellowed, "Hey in there, Cammy, you've got to come out and teach me everything you know about ballet. I mean now. What do I learn first?"

I sank even lower in the tub. Each little knob of my spine bumped along the hard bottom. The warm cloudy water covered all of me like chicken soup. Only my head stuck out. I'd be ecstatic when Luke got over this ballet kick of his!

"Did you hear me, Cammy Wammy?"

"Go away."

He kept on banging. "I shoulda asked Madelaine, that's who I shoulda asked. I bet she would have told me."

"Then why don't you telephone her?"

" 'Cause I don't have her phone number yet, dummy. And I hope she gets the part you want in that ballet."

I bolted upright in the tub. "Whose brother are you, you creep? And you learn first position first. What do you think? First comes before second, doesn't it? Now leave me alone."

"So how do you do it, this first position thing?"

"You have to see it to do it. I can't just tell you."

"Try. I gotta know."

I slid back into the water, braid and all. My face stuck out like one of the stones in the pond in our backyard. Goldfish used to glimmer along its murky bottom before a family of raccoons came down from the foothills and ate up every single fish.

"I gotta know about first position," my brother hollered.

From her bedroom Mom hollered, too. "If only to shut him up, Cammy, answer your brother! Tell him how to do first position."

"Rats!" I grumbled. I sat up shivering. Water wriggled down my shoulders and chest. "Your feet go in a straight line, heels together."

That quieted him for a while. Ten minutes later, though, when I limped into the hall, my braid dripping down the back of my bathrobe, he was waiting at the top of the stairs. He had one heel hooked over the banister.

"Is this right? Is this how you do it?"

I sniffed. "That is not first position."

"I know that! But how come you do this all the time?"

"Well, to stretch. Now get lost."

I headed back the way I had come. And there on the bathroom door glared one of his yellow Post-it Notes. He had not doubled the e but I knew exactly what he meant: "Cameo Cammy ped here!"

"Brat!" I screamed, ripping off the note. He only smirked and, pivoting his pudgy feet in opposite directions, continued his questions. "Is this first position? One foot heads east? The other foot west?"

27

I scowled at his face all blotchy with freckles.

"East and west or north and south. It doesn't matter as long as one toe points left, the other right. But you have to turn out more. No, not from the knees, stupid. From the hips. And your heels should touch."

Actually, though, Luke's position wasn't bad for an absolute beginner. It just wasn't fair. His joints were looser than mine, more like the Paragon's. That's how come her extensions floated so high.

"What comes after first position?" Luke went on.

"Well, second. What do you think?"

Mom's voice shrilled from her bedroom. "Cammy, show your brother second position. Stop acting like a little snip."

I squeezed my lips over my braces. Madelaine was the snip. But I showed Luke second position. And all day Thursday, while I worried about the results of Wednesday's audition, he kept at me to teach him ballet. Which wasn't easy with my leg sometimes still twinging.

By Friday, though, it only hurt if I extended it to the rear. So when school let out Friday afternoon I grabbed my ballet satchel, not only eager to take class but desperate to find out if I would dance Beauty's Little Sister. But when I reached the bus stop, guess who was there teetering, arms airplaning, on the back of the wooden bench? Luke. Being in third grade, he got out an hour earlier than I did and must have rushed right over here.

"Get a load of Luke," yelled Croaker, one of the gaggle of fourth-grade boys straggling along the street, one foot in the gutter, the other on the curb. He got the name Croaker because of how he talks. He lives down the street from us and Mom says he probably has bumps growing on his vocal cords. "What're you trying to be, Luke baby, a wimpy ballet dancer?" Croaker asked.

Luke's face flamed. His fists clenched. "Wimp yourself, Croaker. Bet you can't do this." Luke doubled over, gripped the top of the bench and walked along it on his hands. Now where had he learned that trick?

Except for Croaker and his buddies and, of course, me, everybody at the bus stop applauded. I could have strangled him! Number one, this was my territory. He didn't belong here. It was where I began my three-days-a-week journey to ballet. Number two, he shouldn't be up there on the bench, bothering the three old ladies sitting bunched together like blackbirds on a telephone wire.

Not that they seemed all that bothered. They beamed over their shoulders at him while ducking under his swinging feet.

"Such an agile little fellow," one of them tittered. The other two nodded. "A regular tightrope dancer," said one wearing a wide-brimmed straw hat. The third added, "The darling child reminds me of my great-grandson."

My lips tightened. Here was another example of my brother getting away with murder. "Get down and go home," I ordered. "Daddy expected you an hour ago."

Luke just smirked and didn't spring off the rail until the bus whined to the curb.

I rushed aboard, glad to be rid of him. But he bobbed up the steps right behind me. He dropped a coin into the jangling fare box and charged after me down the crowded aisle.

"I'm going to catch the train with you to San Francisco," he announced.

"You can't come with me. Daddy'll be worried and you don't have a train pass." Which, of course, were not the real reasons. I simply didn't want him horning in on ballet. It belonged to me.

He stuck out his chin. "I'll phone Dad from the depot and I'll pay for the train with the money Grandma sent me for my birthday. So there!"

"Your grandma must be truly proud of a nice boy like you," said the straw-hatted lady from the bus stop. All three had hobbled aboard and, although there was standing room only on the bus, they now perched along the bench directly behind the driver. Other passengers had politely offered their seats. "Here, honey," the lady in the middle told Luke.

29

"we'll squeeze together to make room for you to sit between us."

So Luke sat while I had to stand.

The bus lurched forward. I grabbed the back of a seat to keep from falling. I'd get away from him while he phoned Daddy from the depot. I'd stay in the ladies' room until the train was ready to pull out, then dash aboard just before the doors zipped shut.

From the edge of his seat, Luke watched me, not grinning now. His mouth pouted, soft and full. "And don't you try to ditch me at the train station, Cammy. Not after we get to San Francisco, either. You won't, will you?"

I frowned. Was he some kind of a mind reader to know exactly what I was thinking?

"Of course, she won't, sweetheart," the straw-hatted lady said. "She wouldn't want you to become one of those poor little lost children whose pictures are on milk cartons."

Luke's eyes widened and his lips puckered. But I got him onto the train in San Mateo, off again in San Francisco, onto a crosstown bus, and off with me at the stop nearest the ballet school.

When we arrived in the foyer kids from my class were already pouring out of the dressing room and up the staircase. At the top of it, on the call board, the cast list would be posted for Blikk Eriksen's ballet.

I pointed at a plastic-covered sofa. "Luke, sit!" I said, trying to sound as firm as Mom. "I'll be in the dressing room, then in class. Don't you dare budge until Mom comes to pick us up."

And he seemed to be settling down when Madelaine glided into the foyer. She never walked, instead sort of rolled along as if on skates. Outside the window hummed her Mercedes. Her sharp-nosed chauffeur touched the visor of his cap to her and drove off. Imagine being rich enough to have a chauffeur! She rolled past me like a draft of flower-scented cold air and headed for the stairs.

"Hey, Madelaine, wait up," my brother piped, bounding after her like Foxy bounds after him. She waited, smiling, on the bottom step. "Know what, Madelaine, I'm going to be in your class and learn to dance like Baryshnikov."

I scowled. So he was planning to barge into my class again!

"Luke, come back here and sit down," I snapped. I grabbed for his arm, but missed. "You can't be in our class. For one thing, it's in the professional division and you have to audition to be admitted."

He tossed a rag of hair off his forehead. "I auditioned last Wednesday. And I jumped higher than anybody, didn't I, Madelaine?" He took her hand and, to my surprise, she didn't pull it away. A tiny smile curled her lips. "So will you let me go upstairs with you, Madelaine," he asked, "and be in your class?"

Frowning, nibbling her lips, she eyed the stairs. "I don't know about your taking class, Luke, but I don't think Madame would mind if you just watched."

"She would too mind," I said. "It's against the rules. Haven't you been here even long enough to know that? No visitors allowed except once a year on Parents' Day. Besides, the class is for girls only!"

"Good heavens, Cammy, what's all the shouting about?" Joyce Mallory called, crossing the foyer to us. Joyce Mallory was Blikk Eriksen's girlfriend, also his assistant, who helped him make up ballets and rehearse them. She might even work on *Beauty* and coach me. If I got to dance Beauty's Little Sister, that is.

"Is this the super fantastic jumper Maggie and Blikk told me about?" Joyce asked, laughing. Her laugh soared from the pit of her chest and made you want to laugh, too. Unless you were desperately worried about not getting the part you wanted.

"That's me," Luke said. "The winner of the Super-Duper, Worldwide Easter Bunny Jumping Contest. Wanna see me jump again, Madelaine?" he asked, turning to her.

31

Madelaine was scurrying up the stairs, though, to look at the cast list, no doubt. Which I wanted to do, too, but was afraid my brother would follow me.

Luke's shoulders drooped. "I wanted Madelaine to watch me."

"Why don't you jump for me, sport?" Joyce asked.

Luke grinned. "Good idea. I'll audition for you. And if I jump really high, will you let me be in their class even if it is for girls?"

Joyce laughed. "I'm not promising anything but I'll put in a good word for you with the boss. Go ahead, impress me!"

Beaming, Luke leaped onto the arm of the nearest sofa. From there he sailed from sofa back to sofa back until he landed on the one closest to the front door. Jumping down, he returned to Joyce.

"How was I?"

"Terrific! I can't wait to tell Blikk that I've seen Cammy's brother dance."

Luke planted his feet. "People are always calling me Cammy's brother. But when I'm Lukenikov the Great, that'll all change. Then she'll become just Lukenikov's sister."

Chapter Six

An Incredible Postscript

Entrusting Luke to Joyce, I went to change into my practice clothes. When I passed through the foyer again, Luke, chin in air, was showing her the five ballet positions as if he had invented them. At least, he didn't notice me sneak past. And this would be the very last time he came here. I'd see to that. So would Mom, who hated ballet.

To be extra careful of my leg I took the stairs two at a time, instead of my usual three. My braid, which I hadn't twisted into a topknot yet, thumped the middle of my back in time to my thumping heart. Would I or wouldn't I get to dance Beauty's Little Sister?

At the top of the stairs I halted, too nervous to continue. A dozen yards down the corridor hung the call board. Stapled to it glimmered a sheet of white paper: the computer printout naming the kids in *Beauty*.

But where was everybody? No one bobbed around, craning to see the list. The kids in my class must already have seen it and gone into the studio. I inched down the hall, the leather soles of my technique shoes scritching on the linoleum. Black capitals at the top of the print-out swam together, then cleared to spell out STUDENTS IN *BEAUTY AND THE BEAST*. Smaller letters said, "Story by the Brothers Grimm. Choreography by Blikk Eriksen."

Suddenly my name leaped out at me, abrupt, cropped, short as a punk haircut. It seemed to belong to somebody else. With one finger, I traced the curls of the capitals and the up and down mounds of the m's. Cammy Smith. Me?

In the same line with my name were those of five other girls including Helen. We were all about the same height. Which might be why Helen had been chosen. She hadn't expected to be and must be ecstatic. Three dots joined our names to the parts we would dance . . . Friends and Neighbor Children.

Above our names stretched Madelaine's, her whole, long, elegant name. Madelaine Bettencourt. Opposite it, of course, naturally, shone the words Beauty's Little Sister.

So that was that. I felt hollow, as if all my insides had been scooped out. Defeated by my very own brother's antics at the audition. And by the Paragon's high extensions. Or was it by her highfalutin' name? If I had called myself Cameo Smith, would I have won the part? But I wasn't Cameo. I was Cammy Smith with straight red hair and braces on my teeth. The best dancer in my class, though, until Madelaine showed up.

But what was this? Below the Paragon's name and squeezed between a pair of parentheses was the word "understudy" along with my name. Understudy to Beauty's Little Sister. I sucked in my breath, not knowing whether to be happy or sad. And why the parentheses like an afterthought?

But the real afterthought trailed below the cast list like a postscript at the end of a letter—an incredible P.S. In square, black handwriting somebody—probably Blikk Eriksen—had scrawled "Beauty's Younger Brother . . . Luke Smith."

I let out a yelp and leaned against the cold corridor wall.

Talk about my brother invading my territory! He had taken it over.

"What's wrong?" Helen asked, coming out of our classroom. "You're white as the plaster."

I jabbed a fingertip at Luke's name. "Did you see that?"

"Yeah, I noticed," Helen said, wheezing maybe from shock or maybe because of her allergies. She pushed her glasses higher on her nose. "Looks like your sibling aced you out, Cam. Not to mention me. But I'm happy to be included at all, awful as I am."

"Oh, you're not that awful," I said, although her feet are blobs of bread dough and her balance is utterly hopeless. "Anyway, Helen, about Luke, Mom'll never ever let him be in *Beauty*. Or take ballet, either, like he wants to. He says."

Her eyebrows went up. "Since when? I thought he wanted to be another Joe Montana."

"That was last week. But we'd better go to class. Here comes Madame Harper."

Her earrings jingled up the stairs behind us.

"Congratulations, my darlings!" she said. "So you're both in *Beauty*."

Helen nodded. "I'm practically ecstatic."

Licking my braces, I twisted my braid into its topknot. With Luke here and messing around, I hadn't had time downstairs.

Madame Harper arched a thin, black eyebrow at me. "You don't seem as ecstatic as your friend. You two are among the lucky few. And you, Cammy, are understudying the principal child's role in the ballet."

I rubbed the smudged tip of one of my ballet slippers along a crack between the linoleum squares. The Paragon must have a maid to keep hers so rose petal bright! "But Madelaine's new," I mumbled, frowning, "and yet she's dancing a lead. And my brother, well, he's never had a single ballet lesson in his entire life."

35

"Surely you know that his part is only a walk-on," Madame said. "Blikk won't let him do any dancing."

Which made me a little happier but not much.

"Blikk probably thinks your little brother will be a crowd-pleaser," Madame added. "All that red hair. All that joy and enthusiasm."

I shrugged. "Well, I'm positive Mom won't let him be in it. Besides, by tomorrow he's sure to have lost interest."

"Really, my darling? Because, of course, the child does show considerable talent. As for Madelaine, she may be new, but she had lots of training before she came here. She'll have quite a bit of dancing to do in *Beauty*."

I drew my toe along the crack between the tiles again. I tried to steady my voice. "But after I danced Clara in *Nutcracker* last Christmas, I thought, I mean, I expected . . ."

Madame Harper tilted her shiny, black head. Her bright lips parted in a smile. "Poor Cammy! But *Nutcracker* happened before Madelaine arrived. Also, I understand she danced in *Nutcracker* herself in New York, the role of the Sugarplum Fairy with a children's dance company."

I gasped. The Sugarplum Fairy was the lead in the ballet. I only danced a tiny role, the child Clara. Maggie had performed Clara grown-up.

"So for the first time, my darling, you have some real competition!"

Helen's eyes gleamed behind her glasses. "Formidable competition!"

And for the next hour my competition seemed even more formidable than usual. To begin with, the green ribbon tied around her topknot reminded me of the red one I'd brought but, in my hurry to see the cast list, had left in my ballet satchel downstairs. Rats! During *barre* exercises, working as usual directly opposite the good mirror, the Paragon breezed through every exercise including tracing perfect ovals to the side in *ronds de jambe en l'air*. I, still favoring my leg, struggled even flapping one foot around the other ankle in *frappes*. And my section of mirror reflected me turnip-shaped. During floor exercises, planted in the center of row one, Madelaine spun perfectly balanced double *pirouettes*. In the second row, I strained just to turn singles.

After class ended and we had bowed our thanks to Madame Harper, Madelaine, of all people, drifted over to me. "Uh, Cammy, I was wondering, would you do me a favor?"

I was too surprised to answer. She fluttered a dab of paper in front of me.

"I promised to give this to your brother."

I frowned. "To Luke?"

Her face went pink. "Uh-huh. While you were getting dressed he rushed upstairs but Joyce followed and grabbed him. I didn't have time to give him what he wanted. And now I have to hurry. I'm going to see my mother."

"Your mother? Don't you—don't you live with her?" I stammered. Dumb question. Like the parents of lots of kids, hers were probably divorced. Or at least didn't live together. But I was startled. I mean, she'd hardly said a word to me before.

"Not right now, but she's getting better," Madelaine said. And while I stood staring, not understanding what in the world she was talking about, she said, "Here." She pushed the scrap into my hand and skimmed away. After she left, I unfolded the paper. Seven spidery numbers curled across the page. Her telephone number.

I crumpled the scrap and, forgetting about my leg, dashed after her down the stairs, through the foyer, and out the entrance. At the curb, not waiting for her chauffeur to get the car door for her, Madelaine tugged it open herself and slid in beside him. Weren't passengers supposed to sit in the back?

"Can we stop at MacDonald's and visit her afterward?" Madelaine asked the chauffeur, ignoring or not seeing me on the sidewalk. Before the man could answer, the door closed and the Mercedes glided away.

With my ballet shoes half buried in fallen acacia blossoms,

I stood on the curb, feeling stupid. Why had I rushed after Madelaine? To return the phone number that she, my formidable competition, had given to my brother? I gave a snort and opened my hand. The breeze snatched away the scrap of paper.

Suddenly, a thought hit me. Where was Luke? Neither he nor Mom had been in the foyer when I sped through. They sure weren't out here. I hunched my shoulders. Luke just couldn't have gone off into the city!

He and Mom still weren't in the foyer when I went back inside. But Joyce was beckoning from the doorway of the small first floor studio. She and Blikk Eriksen often coached solo variations in there for roles like Beauty's Little Sister. My heart lifted. Would she tell me that the cast list upstairs was all wrong and that the part I wanted was mine?

I ran to her and waited. She grabbed me in a hug. "Congratulations, doll. Being a Neighbor Child plus understudying Madelaine's role will give you some terrific stage experience. Besides, you'll have a ball."

I pressed my lips over my braces. "But I was sort of hoping . . ." I began, then broke off, afraid my voice would wobble.

"Ah, Cam, honey," Joyce said, cupping my chin, "you wanted the role Madelaine got, didn't you? But she's had more training and . . ."

I didn't hear the rest because in the room behind Joyce stood Luke. Surrounding him, gazing at him, gesturing at him, hovered Blikk Eriksen, Maggie Adams, and, of all people, Mom!

Bending his head toward her, a smiling Blikk Eriksen seemed to be drinking in her opinions like lemonade and she, his. Mom's eyes shone with a kind of wonder, as if dazzled by Prince Charming. Pink splotches colored her cheeks. Her brown eyes gleamed like wet sand. She looked prettier than I'd seen her since she took that job last fall.

"Mom, what are you doing here?" I blurted. "And Luke?"

38

He beamed at the group around him, then, red hair flying, dashed to me. "Didn't I tell you I'm going to be the next Baryshnikov? That's what this huddle's all about. They phoned Mom at work and she said sure I can be in the ballet."

My heart bumped against my ribs. "She wouldn't. I don't believe you."

"Ask her. Just ask her. The man talked and talked about how talented I am. To top it off, he said he'd give me a humongous scholarship, beginning now. And until I catch up with the beginning boys' class, he's going to teach me. Mr. E. himself."

Chapter Seven

Double Trouble

"How could you?" I asked Mom.

She sat in front of me, trying to start Old Faithful.

"How could I what?"

"Let Luke be in *Beauty*, take ballet, everything."

Luke smirked at me over the back of his seat.

" 'Cause I'm going to be the next Baryshnikov, Lukenikov the Great, that's why."

"I asked Mom."

She spun the station wagon away from the curb and around a double-parked car. "Luke's about said it," Mom said. "Your famous Mr. Eriksen thinks your brother could become an outstanding dancer."

"But, Mom," I wailed, "you know how Luke goes from one thing to another. Besides, I thought you and Daddy wouldn't want him to be a dancer because he's a boy."

Mom dodged a truck and made a right-hand turn against a signal. "What's his being a boy have to do with anything? Talent's talent."

The instant we got home Luke bounded ahead of me across the lawn and into the living room.

"Hey, Dad, the big man himself is going to teach me how to dance," he yelled above Foxy's yapping. "Mr. E.!"

40

"His name is Blikk Eriksen. Not Mr. E.," I muttered and pounded up the stairs.

Daddy frowned down at the blue wash flooding his thirsty paper. "That's fine, son," he said, but I knew he hadn't really been listening to Luke. That was the only time he called my brother "son."

"Lloyd, the most extraordinary thing has happened!" Mom said, bursting into the living room. "This Mr. Eriksen, the company's director, believes Luke has great potential as a dancer."

Midway to the second floor I halted, gripped the banister, and peered down. Potential! A psychologist's word, if I ever heard one!

Daddy laid his brush across a mason jar filled with murky blue water. He eyed the painting taped to his board and rubbed a hand through his wispy hair.

"I've heard about Luke's potential before, Alice," he said, not looking up. "His great potential as a major league pitcher when he hurled for a Little League farm team."

"Well, didn't he win the trophy for Best Seven-Year-Old Pitcher of the Year?" Mom asked.

Daddy ignored her question. "His potential as a major poet after he won a local haiku contest. As an archeologist when he dug up a bone Foxy buried in the backyard. So I take his potential as a ballet dancer with several grains of salt." Daddy raised an eyebrow at Mom. "Anyway, I thought you were fed up with ballet."

"Oh, well, I've just been so exhausted—all those off-the-wall kids. And I've been trying to get Cammy to be more realistic about her chances of becoming a professional dancer."

Daddy used his brush to stir the blue water in his mason jar. "Are you sure you're being realistic about Luke's, Alice? Besides, having talent is only the beginning."

Bending over his table, Daddy poked at his watercolor to see if it was dry, then added, "What makes you think Luke will stick to ballet any more than to all the other things he's gone in for?"

"But I will, Dad. This time I will."

"I believe you, bunny," Mom said, calling my brother a name that reminded me of that dumb jumping contest he won in kindergarten. "Lloyd, I've never seen him this keen about anything before. And Mr. Eriksen is so enthusiastic. The school's giving Luke a big scholarship. And with me, money talks."

Daddy looked up from his watercolor. "I've noticed. Did you talk to him about Cammy, too?"

I squeezed the banister. Had she?

"Well, no, but if Cammy has sufficient talent, I'm sure they'll give her a scholarship next year, too, a big one like they're giving Luke."

I doubled myself over the banister and swooped like a cable car down its long, slippery length. At the foot of the staircase I dropped to the floor and rushed to Mom.

"Did Blikk Eriksen actually say I'll get one, Mom? Did he?"

She glanced at me, a frown between her eyes. "Well, no, he didn't. They're short of money, he said. Something about the city cutting funds and private and corporate donors not being as generous as they were before the changes in the tax laws and the big stock market slump."

"But Luke's getting one and he knows nothing about ballet," I wailed.

Mom sighed. "We'll just have to wait and see, won't we? Mr. Eriksen did give the impression, though, that the school is pleased with your work. Quite pleased, anyway. But I guess you have to be at the very top of your class to have a future in ballet. He said you used to be before some girl arrived from New York."

I chewed my braid. The Paragon. My formidable competition! And Luke added to Madelaine meant double trouble.

The next day right before my eyes they joined forces, the New York wonder and my very own brother. We arrived at the ballet school just as Madelaine alighted from her Mercedes.

As usual when Daddy takes us any place, we were late. But Luke could have waited for me instead of tumbling out of our station wagon and scrambling after her. Daddy hadn't even turned off the ignition yet.

Because it was Saturday, he, not Mom, had driven us to San Francisco for our first rehearsal. Mom claimed that she needed the entire day off to rest up. Daddy didn't seem to mind too much. He said it was his turn. Besides, there's a place in the city where he gets his watercolor paper really cheap.

"Hey, Madelaine, wait up!" Luke called, charging across the sidewalk after her. He was wearing jeans, T-shirt, and jogging shoes and planned to rehearse in them, considering practice clothes, especially tights, wimpy. Today he might get by with it because the school dress code wasn't enforced on Saturdays.

Madelaine wore regulation practice clothes even though they weren't required today: pink tights, pink technique shoes, and a black leotard without the back cut out. Some ballet schools allowed students to alter their leotards. Ours didn't.

I sniffed. "Just look at her, Daddy. A real goody-goody. Today she's not even wearing a ribbon to call attention to herself. Maybe she figures she doesn't need one now that she has the role she wants."

Daddy grinned. "Or maybe, Poody Squash, she thinks that following the dress code when nobody else does makes her different enough."

I gave a grunt. I hadn't thought of that.

In the doorway Madelaine wheeled slowly on the mat of fallen acacia blossoms. She smiled. "Hi, Luke. I sort of expected you to phone me last night."

"How could I? You went off and forgot to give me your phone number."

Her glance swept to me. "Then I'll give it to you now, Luke."

Ducking my head, I looked away.

43

"Why in the world does he have to run after that tooth-pick?" I muttered.

Daddy grinned. "Because she doesn't treat him like a kid brother, I suspect. Besides, she's pretty."

I sniffed. "Well, he is a kid brother and acts like one. And I don't think Madelaine's a bit pretty."

Daddy laughed. "Luke does. I admit she's a little thin. Great coloring, though." He squinted, his gaze following the pair through the glass doors and into the foyer. "Amber hair. Ochre and cad-red, I think, with maybe sienna shadows."

I stuck out my lower lip. "Straw-colored with split ends, I'd say. And Luke could have waited for me, his very own sister, instead of racing off with a stranger. He has no idea where the rehearsal is."

"Knowing Luke," Daddy said, "I'm sure he'll find out. Probably from Madelaine."

Daddy was right. By the time I reached the foyer, Luke was jogging up the stairs beside Madelaine. They were smiling at each other, his face tilted up, hers down.

Scowling, I tramped to the dressing room. To take advantage of no dress code, I dragged on red tights and red leotard and tied a red ribbon around my topknot. I'd show Madelaine I wasn't a goody-two-shoes like she was. But when I arrived at the rehearsal studio, Madelaine wasn't there. Neither were Luke or Blikk Eriksen.

"Hurry up, Cam," Joyce called. She didn't break the rhythm she was clapping for *pliés*.

"Where's Mr. Eriksen?" I asked.

"Blikk and I are running separate but equal rehearsals this morning," she said and nodded toward the *barre*. "There's room between Helen and Emily. I'm giving a short warm-up before we begin rehearsing. So get to work, doll."

"But Luke and Madelaine aren't here yet," I said.

"They're not supposed to be here," Joyce said. "Blikk is working with Madelaine and your little brother in one of their scenes with Maggie Adams."

I licked my braces. It wasn't fair. Here I was just one of six while Luke and the Paragon got to work with Maggie and had the good parts. Which they didn't deserve. At least, Luke didn't.

"Actually, Cam," Joyce went on, "since you're Madelaine's understudy you should be there, too. But you learn quickly, so you can pick up the steps later. This morning you need to be here to work on the Neighbor Children's variation. Now grab hold of the *barre* and bend your knees in *pliés*."

Sighing, I grasped the *barre* behind Helen. Like me, she was observing no dress code Saturday but instead of matching practice clothes or even color-coordinated ones, she had on bright green tights and a vivid magenta leotard. I shuddered. Could she be color blind as well as near-sighted?

"Since we have no pianist this morning," Joyce was saying, "I'll clap the beat for you."

I pressed my lips together. Not even any music. While from down the hall floated a waltz to which Luke and Madelaine were probably dancing.

The steps Joyce was teaching were kindergarten stuff, but Madelaine must be learning a variation full of *glissades*, *arabesques*, not to mention *développés*. And Luke's role, although Madame Harper had insisted it was just a walk-on, might include some easy, but fabulous steps Blikk Eriksen had put together especially for my brother. Maybe there also was a nice little *pas de deux* for the two of them that would bring bravos and bravas from the audience while I . . .

"Ahoy, over there, Cammy! Wake up. You're lost," Joyce called. I stared around. How had I ended up on the opposite side of the room?

"Come back and join the party," Joyce said. "You may think skipping is easy, but the timing and patterns are tricky. Your lines cross and re-cross and constantly reverse directions. But tricky timing and complicated patterns never bothered you before. How about concentrating, Cam. And counting. And not daydreaming!"

45

My face flaming, I scurried back to the others.

"Okay, everybody," Joyce continued, "from the beginning again."

I tried, but the waltz music filtering into our classroom was soft, a gentle current, a summer wind on which Luke and Madelaine were floating.

I crashed into Helen.

"Good grief, take it easy!" she said, rubbing her arm. "I thought I was the blind one."

"Sorry," I mumbled.

"Break time," Joyce called. "That means quick drinks of water to help you pull yourselves together. Especially you, Cam. You're just not with it this morning. Must be the fire engine red get-up you're wearing."

I hunched my shoulders.

"Be back in ten minutes, everybody," she added. "And, remember, you're all to head straight downstairs. No lingering in the corridor and bothering the other rehearsal. You know the rules. No kids allowed in the hall while classes or rehearsals are in progress. Okay, ten minutes!"

I hung back while the others crowded out of the classroom. Helen waited in the doorway.

"Cam, if we hurry, we'll just have enough time for diet sodas."

"Go on ahead," I said. "I'm taking it easy on the stairs. My leg, you know."

She wriggled her eyebrows at me. "Sure! Sure!" she said and went along with the rest of the girls.

I waited until they were thumping down the stairs before I dashed toward the music. I had to see what dazzling steps Blikk Eriksen was creating for Luke and Madelaine.

Chapter Eight

A Peeping Thomasina

The hall stretched ahead of me, wide and empty. Nobody was there to remind me that no students were allowed in the corridor or to shoo me downstairs. I followed the waltz music to the next to the last studio up the hall.

Light spilled from the crack where the closed double doors didn't quite meet. The slit was too narrow to see through, but a bright beam of dust swirled out of the keyhole. I bent and peered in.

It was like looking into the peep show I made for social science last year. The teacher said to picture what you wanted to be when you grew up. To see into mine, you spied through a hole I had cut in one end of an empty ballet shoe box. Inside stood a cut-out of Maggie Adams dancing the *Mazurka* from *Les Sylphides*. Her photograph and the backdrop of shadowy forest and *corps* dancers came from *Dance Magazine*. To light the scene I had discarded the lid and pasted thin tissue paper over the top of the box.

Fluorescent ceiling lamps lit the rehearsal studio I was

looking into now. But through the keyhole I could see only the room's center and the mirrors on the opposite wall. A pair of Blikk Eriksens waltzed back to back, one in the room, one in the mirror. Maggie and spindly Madelaine walked behind him, marking the combination he was showing them. Their hands wove in the air to help them remember where the turns and *arabesques* came. I'd been so right! The Paragon did have great steps to dance!

Maggie, too, of course. How lovely she looked, swaying in place, her crinkly hair shimmering in the overhead lights. Beside her and nearly as tall, Madelaine seemed nothing. A stick of candy sucked pale and thin. How could my very own brother think she was pretty?

But where was Larry Randall, the company's leading male dancer? He had the role of the Beast in *Beauty* and must be late for the rehearsal. The awful man had been a real beast when we were both in *Nutcracker*.

I didn't see Luke either until, suddenly, his reflection jumped out at me from the mirror. He wasn't dancing. What he was doing was outrageous even for him. On the other side of the wall from me and a few yards to my left, he was using the *barre* as a balance beam. He toed along it, his arms tilting like the vanes of a windmill.

"Luke, get down," Blikk Eriksen said. He didn't yell or shout. He spoke crisply and quietly, the way a sharp knife cuts. The music stopped.

My breath came fast. Would Blikk Eriksen kick the brat out of the rehearsal? Maybe out of the ballet school? Please, yes!

My eye pressed the keyhole. At the front of the room Madelaine left Maggie's side and scurried to Luke. She reached for one of his hands. "Oh, quickly, Luke. Get down."

"I'm just practicing balancing, Maddy."

I frowned. The Paragon had been in my ballet class for two whole months and none of us called her Maddy. Exactly when had my brother started calling her that? This morning after she gave him her phone number? Letting the wind take it last night hadn't done a bit of good.

Behind Madelaine came Blikk Eriksen, striding directly toward my spying place. I leaped away from the keyhole, my heart thudding. But he headed for my brother.

"Now is not the time for you to practice anything, Luke. Now is the time to watch and learn."

"Okay, Mr. E."

My brother dropped to the floor. He landed on all fours like squirrels did when they dropped out of our oak tree. Only they landed silently. Luke thumped. "Sorry, Mr. E.," he mumbled, probably seeing Blikk Eriksen's raised eyebrow. "I just didn't have anything else to do. When do I get to dance?"

Rubbing his hands together, Blikk Eriksen answered gently, "Luke, yours is not a dancing role."

Relief surged through me. Madame Harper had been right.

"In this ballet," the man continued, "you are supposed to be lame."

My eye bumped the keyhole. Lame? Luke? Who flew everywhere? Up the stairs. Across the blacktop at school. Off our shingled roof to the oak tree.

He pouted. "But I won the Super-duper, Worldwide Easter Bunny Jumping Contest. Besides, I'm a good dancer. You said so yourself. So why can't I dance?"

Blikk Eriksen smiled. "Luke, you have no technique yet. That will come only with good teaching, time, and hard work. But if you concentrate on this little role, you may learn something about acting and about projecting to the audience. You will also pick up some stage experience. But as Beauty's Little Brother you are required only to limp on and off stage leaning on a short crutch."

I gave a sniff. More likely Luke would fling the crutch like one of those Australian boomerangs. Probably at me, especially if Madelaine told him about the phone number incident.

Suddenly behind me a voice barked, "Loitering in the corridors is against the rules, young lady."

I jumped back from the keyhole and up against a pair of long, muscular legs. I let out a little scream and spun around. Above a kind of totem pole of stomach, bulging chest, and enormous jaw glinted two vivid blue eyes. The whole ballet school knew that colored contact lenses made them bluer then they really were. The man was Larry Randall!

"A regular peeping Tom. Beg pardon, a peeping Tomasina. But how'd you expect to go undetected in that bull-baiting red get-up?" he asked, dragging out his words like cowboys do on TV Westerns. The blurb about him in the company's souvenir book said he grew up in Idaho or Montana or some such place.

I inched away from him, staying close to the cold wall.

"I'm—I'm Madelaine's understudy so I needed to see . . ." I began but broke off. No matter what I said he was sure to report me. I edged down the hall toward Joyce's rehearsal. Our ten minute break must have ended fifteen minutes ago.

"Now I know who you are," Randall said. "You're the redheaded brat from *Nutcracker*. Braces and all."

I clamped my mouth over my braces.

He let out a whinny of a laugh, raked his long fingers through his yellow hair, and expanded his nostrils.

How could people consider him good looking? A regular movie star, they said. He must think so, too, or he wouldn't wear sweatshirts and T-shirts with his name stenciled across the fronts three times. Larry Randall. Larry Randall. Larry Randall.

"Uh, I gotta hurry, Mr. Randall. I'm late for rehearsal." I backed away from him.

"Ta-ta, Tomasina," he said and strode into Blikk Eriksen's rehearsal. He was at least an hour late. But I was late, too.

Hunching my shoulders, I rushed down the hall to Joyce's

studio. Would Blikk Eriksen kick me out of *Beauty* when Randall tattled about me being in the hall?

Safely back where I belonged, I almost forgot about Luke and the Paragon. For the first time this morning I enjoyed the skipping combination Joyce was demonstrating. For about the fiftieth time.

"Okay," she said, "let's see if you can get it right now."

But as we repeated it, Blikk Eriksen poked his silvery-gray head into the room.

"I am ready for them," he told Joyce. "How has your morning gone?"

She laughed. "I've seen better, but you might as well take them and try putting it all together. Go along, kids. See you later. Maybe Blikk and the piano will inspire you."

In the new studio with Blikk Eriksen and music, we did do better. Even I skipped in the right direction once I'd made sure that Larry Randall, who was warming up at the *barre*, hadn't told on me. Not yet.

I also checked out Luke, crouching in the middle of the floor. His role actually was only a walk-on!

As for Madelaine, although she had a lovely dancing role, she wasn't really dancing. She didn't sway and swing, swivel her body, and tilt her head like Maggie was doing. Like the music made me, Madelaine's understudy, want to move. If the Paragon couldn't dance this role, I could. And might, the way things were going.

Blikk Eriksen nodded at the pianist to stop playing.

"Madelaine, my dear, you really must feel the music. Dance to it. Let it sing through your body. Try it once more, please."

She nodded, her fingers knotting and unknotting, her gaze sliding sideways first to Larry Randall, then to Luke.

"You can do it, Maddy," my brother told her, his voice going deep.

But when the music began again her dancing was no livelier. Shrugging his shoulders, Blikk Eriksen turned his

51

back on her and walked away. He was always firm about how he wanted his dancers to perform. This was the first time, however, that I had seen him almost annoyed. Was my brother's rotten behavior partly to blame?

Luke sprang up from his crouch and snatched hold of Madelaine's hand. Her glance darted to Randall again. I frowned, puzzled. She seemed petrified of him. And she had never even worked with him. I had, though, in *Nutcracker*.

"Come on, Maddy," Luke said in the same growly voice as before. "Mr. E. means like this."

And lifting his knees, Luke galloped around the room dragging Madelaine after him. Pink spots glowed on her cheeks. A giggle escaped her pale lips. She skipped beside him, letting him swing her hand, looking shy and embarrassed but almost happy.

Blikk Eriksen clapped his hands sharply. The music stopped. So did the spurts of laughter from all over room. People stood like stones. Except for Luke. But even his skipping slowed to a walk.

"Luke, you are not directing this ballet!" Blikk Eriksen said.

Madelaine teetered toward the man, leading Luke behind her like a puppy on a leash.

"Oh, please, Mr. Eriksen, he was only trying to help me."

"That's right, Mr. E., I was just showing Maddy what you wanted."

Blikk Eriksen sighed. "I know you meant well, Luke, but you are completely lacking in self-discipline. All morning you have played the clown, repeatedly disrupting rehearsal. I made a mistake in adding you to the cast. You are not yet ready to be in a ballet."

At the *barre* Randall gave a whinny. "What kid is ready, may I ask? Sonny boy's not even in practice clothes." And continuing his warmup, he thrust forward a leg which looked as thick and strong as a tree trunk.

Luke's glance raced from Blikk Eriksen to Randall and back again. "Okay, after this I'll wear tights, even if they are wimpy. Only please, Mr. E. . . ."

Blikk Eriksen shook his head and pointed toward the door. "You are to leave, Luke. Wait for your sister downstairs."

My brother's head jerked back like at school a couple of weeks ago when Croaker socked him. He marched to the door and dived into the corridor. Madelaine stared after him, twisting her hands.

I chewed my lips. My brother was out of the ballet just as I wanted. So why did I feel as if a soccer ball had smashed into my stomach?

Chapter Nine

A Member of the Family

After the door slammed behind Luke, the studio grew awfully quiet. Ten of us stood around not saying a word. Randall, warming up at the *barre*, was now hoisting his working leg front, side and rear in *grands battements*.

I twisted my braid and, for some reason, felt like crying. Would my brother have enough sense to wait for me in the foyer? He wouldn't wander out of the studio and disappear, would he? I shuddered, remembering the old ladies on the bus talking about the pictures of lost children on milk cartons.

"Very well, back to work," Blikk Eriksen said. "Your skipping variation follows the Vision Scene. In it, Beauty sees the Beast dying of loneliness in his castle. She pities him and decides to return to marry him. Bidding the children farewell, she skips and dances with them. We will run through it now."

Did we ever! A dozen times at least. The pianist started and stopped, started and stopped, mainly because, with Luke gone, the Paragon had stiffened up again.

Finally, shaking his head, Blikk Eriksen said, "Enough skipping. Now the Neighbor Children wave their goodbyes and wander off, exiting right."

We scattered toward the edges of the studio which, during these early rehearsals, served as wings. We lined up along one of the *barres* while Blikk Eriksen explained the next scene to Maggie and Madelaine.

"The Neighbor Children have gone now and Beauty says goodbye to her little brother and sister. To her little sister, I should say, since we have eliminated the little brother."

Madelaine wet her lips. Her voice trembled. "But, Mr. Eriksen, how can you just get rid of him? A member of the family?" she asked, tears shimmering in her eyes.

A snort of laughter came from Randall, who now had a thick bony ankle on the *barre* and was stretching his legs. Awful as he was, I almost laughed with him. Having Luke as a member of the family wasn't exactly the greatest, especially lately, since the creep had started calling himself Lukenikov. He even wrote that name on his math and spelling papers. To bug his teacher, no doubt. Also to worry Betsy, our school psychologist, who phoned Mom night after night to discuss, psychologist to psychologist, what motivated his behavior. I could have clued them in. One huge case of inflated ego!

"Madelaine, I am sorry that you are upset by Luke's absence," Blikk Eriksen said gently. "But, as I said before, he is not yet ready to perform."

"Thank heavens for that," I whispered to Helen who leaned against the *barre* beside me.

She nodded. "It's me they should eliminate. Me and my hay fever and cloddy feet."

"Oh, for gosh sakes, Helen, don't be such a sad sack. Lighten up and watch Maggie dance."

Maggie and Madelaine were rehearsing their farewell *pas de deux*, Maggie on *pointe*, Madelaine only on half *pointe*. In New York the Paragon had been allowed to start *pointe*

55

work. At least, that was what Luke told me the other day, bragged to me.

"Yay, yay," he sing-songed. "That's cause Maddy's a better dancer than you, Cameo Cammy!"

"She is not," I told him, ignoring the name he had called me. "She's only studied longer. Besides, out here, Madame Harper took away Madelaine's *pointe* shoes. The Paragon hadn't taken class for a year and her feet sickled. No way was she ready for *pointe* work, Madame said. No more than the rest of us in Class Two."

So since the role of Beauty's Little Sister didn't require *pointe* work, I should be performing it, not just understudying it. I sure wouldn't dance this variation the way the Paragon was, stiff as the Doll in *Petrouchka*. Her *arabesque* poked straight up behind her like a radio antenna. Her narrow feet stabbed the *bourrées* up and down, up and down, like the needle on Mom's old sewing machine. And, although I hated Randall at least as much as Madelaine seemed to, I would never, while dancing, dart scared glances at him like she kept doing.

A sudden, resounding clap halted the music.

"Madelaine, do not look at the Beast," Blikk Eriksen said. "In this scene he is a vision which only Beauty can see. And, my dear, this is not a contest to see how high you can push your *arabesque*. Or how fast you can *bourrée*. Your sister Beauty is going away. How do you think you would feel if your real sister were leaving home forever?"

Madelaine's cheeks grew red. She stared down at her shoes, pink as rose petals.

"I don't have a sister," she whispered, her eyes shifting toward Randall and away again.

"Do you have a brother then?" Blikk Eriksen asked.

She shook her head.

"A friend?" he said. "A best friend perhaps?"

Tears shone in her eyes. "Not any more. Not since Luke left."

56

Frowning, Blikk Eriksen walked in little circles. He cleared his throat. "Well, Madelaine, I have tried to explain why I asked Luke to leave. Now I want you to forget him and concentrate on this ballet. Imagine that you are losing someone very dear to you. Someone you love very much. A father. A mother. Or," the man added with a laugh, "perhaps, even Luke. You must project your emotions, my dear, and show the audience how unhappy you are to be losing your beloved sister. Do you think you can do that?"

"I don't know," she whispered, glancing at lanky Randall again.

A snicker came from him. "Like I keep saying, Eriksen, kids and ballet don't mix!"

Shaking her head at Randall, Maggie put an arm around Madelaine's shoulders. "Of course, you can do it, honey." She turned to Blikk Eriksen. "I really think she can, Blikk."

Rubbing his hands together, Blikk Eriksen sighed. He nodded toward the piano. "Once more, please."

But before the pianist could strike the first note, Larry Randall made a sudden dash to the double doors. He slammed one open against the studio wall. Plaster crumbled onto the floor. I caught my breath. For out in the dimly lighted corridor Luke staggered backward and blinked into the bright studio.

Randall grabbed him by a shoulder and shook him like Foxy shook squirrels and raccoons when he could catch them. My brother's chin jutted forward, but his face was so pale that his freckles stood out like splotches of catsup.

"Oh, poor Luke," Madelaine said.

Luke must have heard. He gave her a trembly grin.

Randall snickered. "Peeping through the keyhole, weren't you, buddy boy? The second peeping Tom I've encountered today." He raised a yellow eyebrow at me. "The first was a peeping Tomasina."

I ducked my head, detesting him. Would he tell Blikk Eriksen now?

"Luke, I asked you to wait downstairs," Blikk Eriksen said. "Why were you in the corridor?"

My brother sucked in his lips. Then sliding a glance at the Paragon, he answered in a voice nearly as soft as hers. "I didn't want to miss anything, Mr. E. In case—in case you let me back in your ballet."

For a minute even the air, heavy and smelly with sweat and baby powder, seemed to listen. Helen wheezed. Madelaine let out a long, quavery sigh. I frowned. Would Blikk Eriksen believe Luke and let the little faker return?

Larry Randall whinnied. "A likely story!"

But Blikk Eriksen smiled. "Let go of the boy, Randall. And, you, young man, listen carefully. I will take you back mostly for Madelaine's sake. She seems to think she needs you."

Randall gave a grunt. "Holy Toledo! What is this, a clinic for disturbed children?"

"But no more puckish behavior," Blikk Eriksen said. "The next time you so much as blink inappropriately, out you go for good."

I pressed my lips tight over my braces. So Luke had won! As usual!

"Oh, he'll behave," Madelaine bleated, sounding more like a baby goat than a girl nearly thirteen who was getting bosoms. I scowled at her. What right had she to make promises for my brother?

An hour later, when Blikk Eriksen dismissed us, Luke and the Paragon rushed off together. They were giggling hysterically at the top of the stairs by the time Helen and I came out.

I frowned. "What's Luke up to now?"

"Look," Helen said and pointed to the studio door. One of Luke's yellow Post-it Notes fluttered just above the keyhole. I gasped. The two of them had figured out what Randall had on me. The words, spelled correctly, with Madelaine's help, no doubt, said. "Tomasina spied here!"

Chapter Ten

Randall's Rotten Childhood

"Run along now, my darling," Madame Harper called to Madelaine. Monday's class was nearly over. For the past two weeks we had been rehearsing *Beauty* not only on Saturdays but also after class on Mondays, Wednesdays, and Fridays.

"Head high, Madelaine," our teacher went on. "Don't look so frightened. Blikk simply asked me to let you out of class a little early to rehearse."

Madelaine hovered near the *barre*, blotting her skinny neck and shoulders with a towel. "Who'll be there?" she asked. "Maggie? Will Mr. Randall?"

"She has a real phobia about Randall," Helen whispered beside me. We were waiting for Madame Harper to demonstrate another part of the variation we had been preparing all year for the *Window on the Future* demonstration program. "She's as terrified of him as you are."

I sniffed. "Who says I'm terrified? Not that he doesn't try to scare me. I just hate his guts. Always making nasty remarks about me during *Nutcracker* rehearsals." I didn't mention the bit about his catching me at the keyhole a couple of weeks ago.

Madame Harper swung her earrings impatiently. "All I know, Madelaine, is that you are to go. Now."

The Paragon shot a sideways look at me and Helen. "Shouldn't the others come too?"

Helen's mouth tucked into its half-grin. "Safety in numbers."

"The others will come later," Madame said. "As soon as class finishes. Blikk wants only you and the little boy now."

"The superstars," I muttered.

"Oh, then Luke will be there, too," Madelaine said, her voice lifting a little.

"Yes. Yes. Now hurry along. Don't keep Blikk waiting."

Madelaine skittered out the door, leaving a breath of her flowery perfume behind her.

When class ended, the other six of us hurried to the rehearsal studio. Randall was there, worse luck, already working with Maggie on the Vision Scene. So were my brother and the Paragon, but while the principals danced the *pas de deux* Luke and Madelaine only had to cling together.

They soon ran into the wings and joined the rest of us to await Randall's exit. When it came, it was a near disaster. Instead of moving directly offstage, he angled left and plowed smack into us.

And, although he didn't actually bump Madelaine like he did me, she paled, squeaked, and shrank against my brother.

"Why don't you watch where you're going?" Luke growled at Randall.

"Yeah, why don't you?" I blurted. "You could have hurt somebody. Me, for instance."

"Oh, I do beg your pardon," Randall said, sarcastic. "But, watchful as you usually are, didn't you spy me coming, Tomasina?"

I stiffened. Tomasina again. And spy. He might as well come right out and blab everything.

"Eriksen," Randall complained, "they were blocking my exit. And may I make a suggestion? Instead of real live children why not use small members of the *corps de ballet?* At least, they're professionals, not always underfoot."

Blikk Eriksen quietly closed his thick notebook. "These children are the artists of tomorrow, Randall. They need to gain stage experience."

Randall grunted, poked his movie star profile toward the ceiling, and, elbows angled back, sagged against the *barre*.

A few nights later a similar scene occurred. It began just after we had arrived in the rehearsal studio. The school secretary puffed in to fetch the Paragon. "There's a phone call for you, dear."

Madelaine and Luke stared at each other. Her fingers wove together.

"Don't worry, Maddy," he growled, his voice going so deep he sounded almost grown-up. "Everything'll be okay."

"What'll be okay?" I asked him after she had scurried out the door. "What's wrong?"

He shrugged. "Search me."

I grabbed him by an arm. "Don't give me that. You know everything about her. You two are always on the phone."

Which was true. Every night if he didn't call her, she phoned him. One night at the ballet school, though, I heard her say, "Not tonight, Luke. We have to go see her."

I had frowned. Who was "her"? Madelaine's Mom? For that matter, who did "we" include besides Madelaine? Her father? She'd said she didn't have any brothers or sisters.

"Listen, Luke," I said, "I saw how Madelaine looked at you before she went to answer the phone. Has something bad happened, to her mother maybe?"

"How should I know?"

"You know. And what about her mom, anyway?"

He shrugged again.

"Is she sick or something?" I asked.

"It's none of your bees wax," he said and barged to the door to meet Madelaine who was just returning. They buzzed together for a second or two. But I never did find out what the phone call was about.

Blikk Eriksen clapped his hands for attention. "Is everybody here now? Fine!"

Randall grunted. "Isn't this delightful! A child-oriented production! Rehearsals can't begin until the very last little toddler toddles in."

Madelaine's eyes grew round. Luke clenched his fists and glared at Randall, challenging him as if Randall were Croaker's size and not six feet tall and muscular.

"Your brother would take on the world for that toothpick," Helen whispered beside me at the *barre*. "Talk about David and Goliath!"

"We begin with the Vision Scene," Blikk Eriksen went on, ignoring Randall. "Positions, everyone. Randall and Maggie at center stage, please. Luke and Madelaine, downstage left."

The scene began okay. Maggie stretched into a lovely, long *arabesque* on *pointe*. Randall steadied her. He lifted her and poised her on his shoulder. But from there, things fell apart. Instead of lowering her slowly into another *arabesque*, he plunked her on the floor like Mom plunks a grocery sack on the sofa. He tromped to Luke and Madelaine and nudged them stage left.

"What does the big bully think he's doing?" I whispered to Helen. "Shoving kids around."

Not that I didn't push Luke around myself lots of times and feel like pushing around the Paragon whenever I saw her. But I wasn't a grown-up like Randall. I was just a kid like they were.

Randall pointed left. "You kids are supposed to stand there. Can't you see the 'x' chalked on the floor?" He

62

pivoted to Blikk Eriksen. "Eriksen, I won't have them between me and the audience, stealing my scenes."

I licked my braces. It was the *Nutcracker* rehearsals all over again. Almost every night I used to rush out to Old Faithful in tears and complain to Mom all the way home.

"Sounds like he has a few problems himself, Cammy," she said. "Must have had a rotten childhood."

Madelaine clung to Luke, whose chin barely reached her shoulder.

"Fathead!" Luke muttered, glaring at Randall.

During the ride home that night, with Mom grumbling about how late rehearsals always ran, I asked Luke, "Didn't you see the 'x'?"

" 'Course, dummy. Do you think I'm blind as Helen?"

"Then how come you weren't where you belonged?"

Luke tossed a scrap of red hair off his forehead. "Randall had it coming. After I become Lukenikov the Great, you better believe I'll never let that jerk on the same stage with me."

I sniffed, and Mom said to Luke, "Bunny, I have to admire your modesty. Future fame has not gone to your head."

Chapter Eleven

The Big Moment

As opening night approached and rehearsals moved downtown to the theater Madelaine became more and more jittery. So did I, of course. Not as jittery as Madelaine, though. She twisted her fingers until I thought they'd break off and every day she seemed paler. Maybe her veins had always showed through blue, but now her skin seemed as thin and clear as porcelain.

But at dress rehearsal the night before *Beauty* opened, she looked almost calm. At least, she certainly seemed calmer than I was downstairs in the icy dressing room we all shared. Except Luke. His was at the end of the hall. Had she finally become a little bit confident with rehearsals going well and with him always at her side? He acted as if he were her brother, not mine.

Upstairs, though, when the brass and percussion sections began rumbling the Beast's theme, she clutched his arm. They stood near me in the shadowy first wing. Helen and the other Neighbor Children were waiting closeby in the second wing.

Then Randall sauntered under the stage lights. Horns sprouted from his head. A long, thick tail switched between his legs. "I can't do it, Luke. I can't," Madelaine whispered, reaching for my brother.

A shudder went through me. Randall in the hideous costume brought back all the terrors of *Nutcracker*. Maybe that was why I snapped at Madelaine. "Look, you're not the only one with a few butterflies!"

Luke shoved himself between us. "Leave her alone, dummy. Can't you see she's having a hard time?"

"What is she? The Princess and the Pea or something?" I asked. "More sensitive than the rest of us?"

"Yes, she is."

"Then she shouldn't plan on being a dancer."

"You don't understand anything, stupid idiot sister! She wants to be a dancer as much as you do!"

"It's all right, Luke," Madelaine said, brushing frizzes of hair off her forehead as if they were cobwebs. "Since she's your sister, I don't mind telling her. It's because he—Mr. Randall—reminds me of someone. The teacher my mother found for me in New York. Not a good teacher, I know now, but he convinced her he would turn me into a ballerina overnight. When she wasn't around, though, he was always putting me down. In class, and especially when he directed *Nutcracker*. He was also the one adult in the cast. Drosselmeier."

I started. So like me, Madelaine not only had danced in *Nutcracker*, she had had problems with a man in the ballet. But her man had danced the mysterious magician Drosselmeier, not the Nutcracker Prince as Randall had.

She ducked her face into her thin hands. "He was the reason—one of the reasons—I quit dancing."

Luke patted her arm. "Take it easy, Maddy," he said, his voice deepening. "All that happened ages ago. And you only quit for a year. When you moved out here you found this great school. So forget all that. Like my mom says, 'Remembering makes things seem lots worse than they were.'"

I rubbed my tongue over my braces. It was easy for Luke

65

to say, "Forget it!" But I hadn't forgotten my *Nutcracker* and obviously Madelaine hadn't forgotten hers.

"I know I shouldn't think about it, Luke," she said. "But he was always telling me I'd never be a dancer, then in the middle of the battle with the mice he rolled his huge, black-outlined eyes and muttered how hopeless I was. That's when I ran offstage and got my mother so upset."

Madelaine's thin fingers fluttered down the front of her lacy costume. In the darkness it glimmered pure white beside my ruffled dark green costume. Mine was the same as those worn by all the other Neighbor Children.

"Anyway, Maddy, I'm with you now so everything'll be okay. Come on. That's our cue." Luke pulled her into the bright lights.

Randall was staggering over the entire stage, grasping at the air. But Madelaine seemed calm until he made a sudden lunge and clawed at her face. She drew back and his laugh roared above the Beast's rumbling theme music.

"I don't remember the clawing bit before," Helen said, ducking around the flat that separated her wing from mine.

"He's improvising, the creep," I said, shivering. "He did that in *Nutcracker*, too. Remember? Made claws of his hands and jabbed them at me just before snatching off his nutcracker mask and turning into the prince. A joke, he said. I didn't think so."

"Neither does Madelaine," Helen said. "Good grief, she's about to faint!"

Madelaine didn't faint but clung to Luke while Randall soared away in a series of *tours jetés*. In the middle of one he thudded to the floor and stalked to the footlights. His nostrils flaring, he bellowed into the auditorium, "Eriksen, do something about that girl. She'll ruin everything. Look at her. Limp as a tassel."

I pressed my lips together. I was almost as limp.

Blikk Eriksen rushed across the ramp that during rehearsals connected the auditorium to the stage.

"All right, everybody, take ten minutes. Come, my dear," he said and led Madelaine past Helen and me.

"I can't do it, Mr. Eriksen," the Paragon kept saying. "I can't. I can't."

"Sure you can, Maddy," Luke said, bounding after them.

Blikk Eriksen sat her down on a costume box. "Rest a little, my dear. Have a soda. Talk to your friend Luke. Afterward you will be fine."

Madelaine shook her head. "No, I'll ruin everything like I did in New York."

"You won't, Maddy," Luke said, dropping down beside her. "You'll be great!"

"You will do beautifully," Blikk Eriksen said. "Please try to calm her," he added to Joyce, who had followed him across the bridge from the auditorium.

"The boss is right," Joyce said. "Just dance, Madelaine. Forget about Randall."

"Yes," Maggie Adams said, coming offstage and kneeling beside Madelaine. "Randall's bark is lots worse than his bite."

"No," Madelaine moaned. "He's right. I'll ruin everything even if he—Drosselmeier—isn't here. And my mother will be out front like in New York. It was Christmastime," she went on, her voice a thin thread. "When I ran out of the theater all the trees were lit up, and the night was filled with Christmas carols. And I was crying."

I hunched my shoulders. She seemed so afraid. Afraid of Randall. Afraid of the teacher in New York. But especially afraid of her mother coming. My mom was coming, too. And, although she wasn't exactly enthusiastic about my dancing, I wasn't scared of her watching me. Worried, maybe. Not terrified the way Madelaine seemed to be.

Blikk Eriksen bent over her again. "Pull yourself together, my dear. We must continue."

"Come on, doll," Joyce begged. "It's almost eleven o'clock

and before we can quit tonight we have to run through the rest of the ballet."

But Madelaine kept shaking her head. "I can't. I can't."

Finally, Blikk Eriksen stood up, sighing. "Take care of her, will you?" he asked Joyce.

"You don't have to," Luke told Joyce in a surprisingly deep voice. "I will." He wrapped his arms around the Paragon.

Blikk Eriksen smiled. "Good," he said, then turned to me. "All right, Cammy. Since you are Madelaine's understudy, please take your place onstage."

A shiver ran through me. This was what I wanted, wasn't it? To take over Madelaine's part. To dance the starring kid's role in *Beauty and the Beast*. So why did this lump fill my throat?

Behind me Luke grunted. "Hope you're happy. You finally got what you've been dying for. Poor Maddy's role!"

Chapter Twelve

The Understudy

"But it wasn't my fault Madelaine couldn't dance it," I cried.

I licked my braces, wondering if maybe I was somehow to blame. Until now I had wanted her role so badly.

"Come on, doll. This is your big moment," Joyce said. "Your lucky break. So stop chewing your braid and get onstage."

I dropped the end of my braid as if it were burning me. My heart rattled in my chest.

"But I can't wear Madelaine's costume!" I cried.

"No excuses, kiddo. Onstage now, please."

"But I'll never ever be able to get into that hankie. She's miles taller and skinnier."

"Never mind the costume, Cam. We'll worry about that later. For now, wear what you have on."

I stared down at the layers of dark green ruffles. "This old thing?"

Joyce laughed. "That old thing. Just get out there."

She and Blikk Eriksen recrossed the ramp to their seats and Maggie led me onstage into the blue haze of the gels. "You'll do fine, honey," she whispered.

"Take it from bar thirty," Blikk Eriksen called to the conductor. "Cammy, Beauty's vision of the Beast has vanished. The Neighbor Children have exited. And Beauty, before returning to the castle to marry the Beast, is saying goodbye to her little sister and brother. But where is the little brother? Onstage, please, Luke!"

I turned to look for Luke but he was no longer sitting on the costume box. He wasn't in the wings at all. Not onstage, either. And neither was Madelaine. Both had vanished.

I frowned. They had probably only gone downstairs to the dressing rooms. But I kept remembering the old lady on the bus and what she'd said about snapshots of lost children on milk cartons. I dashed to the wing where Helen was waiting.

"Did you see where they went?"

She shook her head. "How could I? Joyce made me leave my glasses downstairs. People in fairy tales don't wear glasses, she said. Everybody in them has twenty-twenty vision."

Backstage was dim and shadowy. Luke and Madelaine could be anywhere. Especially if they were hiding on purpose. I'd played hide and go seek with Luke often enough to know he could blend into the thinnest shadow, fit behind the narrowest tree trunk.

"Luke Smith, onstage, please," Joyce called over the loudspeaker.

But Luke didn't show up.

"See what I mean about kids and ballet?" Randall drawled from the stage. "They're antithetic!"

"Loosely defined, antithetic means that kids and ballet don't belong together," Helen was explaining to me when Joyce loped across the bridge to the stage.

"Oh, dry up, Larry!" she snapped. "Maybe we could find him if we had a little light. Let's have the working lights, please."

A white glare flooded the entire stage area. Adults and kids spread out looking in back of scenery, costume boxes,

70

curtains, anything large enough for Luke and/or Madelaine to hide behind, under, or on top of.

I rushed downstairs to the dressing rooms. Neither of them was in the girls'. Nor in Luke's. But on his door shone a huge ragged scrap torn from the shelf paper that lined the dressing tables. Shaped sort of like a star, it carried the message, "Lukenikov the Great stared here!" Starred, he meant. But what did knowing when to double consonants matter now? A sob caught in my throat. I'd wring the little brat's neck? If—when—I found him!

Up the stairs I sprinted and past all the people milling about. I dashed by the security guard, then turned back.

"Have you seen my brother?" I asked him. "Short. About to my chin. Red hair. Freckles. Maybe with a girl. Skinny. Blond. Taller than me."

"Going or coming?" the man asked, chewing on a toothpick.

"Well, going."

The man shook his head. "I only check people coming in. Sorry."

I grunted. Big help he was! I darted to the stage door and out. The night hung low and gray. Wind shook the tops of the trees bordering the curb and sailed tatters of fog past the sharp lines of the skyscrapers.

"Luke, where are you?" I yelled into the mumble of traffic and general city noises.

No answer. I hurried down the broad concrete steps to the street, shouting his name. The buildings, shooting straight up all around me, called back, "Luke, Luke." If he had disappeared into one of those black streets, those gorges, maybe with Madelaine, maybe not, would anybody ever find him?

A man sauntered past, not in rags really, but in pants miles too big and a long, stained jacket that flapped in the wind. He might just be someone with no place to live, but his eyes sagged as if weighted down and set my heart rumbling. I sped faster, looking over my shoulder at the man.

71

That's when I plowed into someone. A squeak burst from me.

"Look where you're going, dummy."

"Luke!" I cried and grabbed him into a hug. I pushed him away again fast. "Where have you been, you little creep? Disappearing when you're supposed to be rehearsing. You know what Blikk Eriksen told you! And Mom and Daddy are due here any minute to pick us up. I could just strangle you. Come on, everybody's waiting."

He pounded off. "Then let's get going."

I scrambled after him. "Wait for me. Exactly where have you been?"

"Where do you think? Seeing that Madelaine got out to her car okay. There she goes now."

He waved at the Mercedes, which like a white shadow eased away from the curb, U-turned, and slipped into the fog. We returned to the theater, Luke scampering ahead.

"Here I am, Mr. E.," he announced, spurting onto the stage. "I knew you'd want to be sure Madelaine got to her car okay."

An explosion sputtered over the loudspeaker. Blikk Eriksen laughing and trying not to, it turned out. "Thank you, Luke. Joyce, everybody, the lost is found. We now begin where we were about half an hour ago. Cammy, you know the *pas de deux*," he said.

Or did he ask? The Norwegian way Blikk Eriksen tilted his voice at the ends of sentences always left me wondering if he was asking or telling you something. Going onstage, I was still trembling and out of breath.

The orchestra began Beauty's theme music. It was the same thin, sweet waltz I'd heard so often floating down the corridor at the ballet school. In the theater dozens of violins, cellos, woodwinds, plus a single harp swelled the melody.

I drew in a shaky breath. But after watching the *pas de deux* dozens of times, I had to know it, didn't I?

Maybe guessing all my worries, Maggie whispered, "Relax, Cammy. You found your brother and I'll talk you through the variation."

She took my right hand in her left. "*Bourrée* to the right," she said. But I knew. I already knew. The music sang the steps to me. I floated beside Maggie and closed my feet in a neat *assemblé*. Then together we drifted back the way we had come.

"Now, *bourrée* to the left," she said.

I nodded, smiling. The music carried me along. No need to count. Just ride the music. At our feet crouched a small boy in a blue velvet suit. A crutch lay on the floor beside him. Except for that pointy chin and thatch of carroty hair, he might have been a cherub in one of Daddy's Italian art books. Not Luke!

"Cammy, take my hand," Maggie said. "Wrist firm. Now stretch into *arabesque*. Good girl. Lovely. Nice and high. Now *plié* into a deep *penché*. Push your *arabesque* higher. Higher, honey." Her eyes and lips were smiling.

I was smiling, too. Then it happened. The sudden, sickening tear in my left thigh, the same hamstring I had pulled before. I groaned. My leg jerked but I didn't lower it, not until the music changed for more *bourrées*. My leg hurt, though, a whole lot. And when the steps repeated, I would have to *penché* again and extend my leg into another *arabesque*.

"Higher," Maggie coached. "As high as last time, Cammy."

I stretched my leg higher, higher. I moaned and chewed my lips. Pain. Pain. Pain.

"That's the way, Cammy," Maggie whispered. "Now one more time, the *bourrées*. That's it. Great!"

And she slid away to help Luke to his feet. She handed him his crutch and he and I joined the crowd in the wings, he trying to hobble, I trying not to.

"You weren't too bad!" he said. "Not absolutely terrible, I mean."

I pushed out my chin. "Maggie said I was great!"

73

"Not as great as Maddy would have been. Your first *arabesque* was okay, but the second one was puny! Not scraping the ceiling like Maddy's would have! If only that big shot Randall hadn't terrified her."

"Was it my fault she couldn't take a joke?" Randall's voice drawled behind us. "And speaking of jokes, your being here is one," he told me. "You should be at home with an ice pack."

I sucked in my breath. How had he known I'd pulled a hamstring?

Randall snickered. "Should it get around that you're prone to injuries, scratch your chances for a scholarship next year, Tomasina!"

I shuddered. Tomasina again!

Giving a whinny of a laugh, he strode away on his long, muscular legs.

"Does it hurt much?" Helen asked, coming up beside me. So she had noticed, too! Had absolutely everybody? She offered me an ice pack from the insulated chest kept backstage for emergencies.

"I don't need any ice," I said. "It's nothing. Hardly hurts at all. A twinge maybe. It'll be okay by tomorrow."

But the next morning, the morning of opening night, I could hardly get out of bed.

Chapter Thirteen

Cammy Smith
Danced Here!

Trying to climb out of bed the next morning, I groaned. My poor leg. Get to the shower, I thought. A good, hot shower! Gently, I lowered my feet to my braided rug and tottered down the cold hall to the bathroom. Although fogged up and smelling of Ivory Soap and spicy after-shave lotion, it was now miraculously empty.

Mom must be halfway up Highway 280. Daddy would have set cereal, juice, and milk on the kitchen table for Luke's and my breakfasts. Now he'd be in the living room already enveloped in the haze that wraps him like cotton when he paints.

I limped to the tub. My leg might have hurt less crawling into a stall shower but there wasn't one in this whole, sprawly house with its tower and half dozen peaked roofs. That was one of the projects Mom had for Daddy: build a downstairs bathroom with an honest-to-goodness stall shower!

I lowered myself into the tub, first my good leg, then the bad. Hot water gushed out of the faucet and, after I pulled up

75

the lever, rained down from the shower head. Teetering on my good leg, I dried off and got into my clothes. The shower had eased the pain but I had to hang onto the banister and stiff-leg it down the stairs.

At the bottom grinned Luke. "Hurt your leg last night, didn't you? Want to borrow my crutch from the ballet?"

"No thank you!"

He smirked. "We could switch roles. You be the little lame brother. I'll dance Maddy's part with the sky-high *arabesques*."

"As if you could!"

Then I sighed. How in the world would I manage them myself?

With ballet classes cancelled today because of opening night, we didn't have to rush to San Francisco right after school. Daddy drove us, but not until really late when he finally reached a good stopping place in his watercolor. He delivered us to the theater one hour after we were supposed to have been there, then zoomed off. He should have met Mom forty-five minutes ago. They were having dinner before coming to see the ballet.

"Me first. Me first," Luke squawked when we both tried to push backstage at the same time. Shoving me into the door frame, he yelled, "Hey, Cammy Wammy, you're still limping!"

He bounded past me and the security guard. On the stairs down to the dressing rooms he turned to face me, hitching his weight from hip to hip. "Step, shift. Step, shift," he said. "That's how you've been walking all day. Don't think I didn't see you at recess just 'cause I was on the other side of the blacktop playing soccer. You were tottering around like an old grandma. Still are!"

"Children!" snapped a woman seated outside the dressing room I shared with the other girls in *Beauty*. "Keep your voices down, please." She was Claire's mother and had volunteered to make sure that all of us got to the wings in time for our entrances.

"You're both late," she said, looking up from something purple she was knitting. "You missed the warm-up class. Hurry now and get changed. And you, young man, don't go in there. That's the girls' dressing room. You're to change down the hall."

Luke made owl eyes at me and pranced off. " 'Course! What else? The star dressing room for Lukenikov the Great!"

"Lukenikov, Kukenikov!" I muttered.

"Children, children," warned Claire's mother.

"Sorry," I said and ducked past her and into the dressing room. I rounded my shoulders against its practically zero degree cold. Glaring white, it was an igloo burrowed under the hills of San Francisco.

"How's the hamstring, Cam?" Helen asked.

I tightened my lips. "Fine. Just fine." And, trying not to hobble, I edged to the place she had saved next to hers at one of the room's two dressing tables. The other girls from our class already sat along it in their ruffled green costumes. Their faces were clown-like under white powder and red rouge.

I eased my rear end onto a chair so small and rickety that its pencil-thin legs shivered under me.

"What'd your physician say?" Helen asked, blinking at me. Her glasses sat among the powder puffs and makeup tubes in front of her. Without them, her eyes were wide and staring as if trying to focus on something.

"Who needs a doctor?" I asked. "I'm perfectly okay. In lots better shape than the Paragon was yesterday."

Helen elbowed me. "Hush. She's back. Over there."

I caught my breath. For there all alone at the second dressing table drooped Madelaine. Had she heard what I said? Not that I cared a whole lot but it would be embarrassing. Besides, last night I'd felt a little sorry for her with Randall pulling on her some of the same rotten tricks he'd

77

pulled on me. She didn't look up. She had on one of the ugly green costumes the Neighbor Children had to wear.

"Why's she wearing that?" I asked.

"She's your replacement."

"Mine? How come?"

"Because, silly, with you doing her part, somebody has to do yours. Joyce finally got hold of her on the phone a little while ago and asked her."

"And the Paragon agreed to do it?"

"She's here, isn't she? I guess she figured it's so easy that she couldn't possibly mess up in front of her mother no matter what antics Randall pulls. Or maybe Joyce twisted her arm a little. Mentioned that a scholarship next year might depend on her cooperation."

I sniffed. "As if she needed one!"

Helen shrugged. "Anyway, she's here and applying her makeup. Which you'd better start doing too."

At the second table Madelaine craned toward the mirror, smearing white gunk on her face. To save time we had skipped making up for last night's dress rehearsal. I reached for a tube. "Wish I knew how to put on this stuff."

"Joyce did mine," Helen said. "She'll probably come help you sooner or later."

"How come Madelaine's doing her own?" I asked.

"She must have learned how when she was with the children's company in New York. Get started, Cam, it's almost time for the ballet to begin."

I glanced frantically around. "Oh, where's Joyce?"

"Don't panic, doll," Joyce said, swooping into the room. "I'm here. And I've brought your costume."

Swinging a coat hanger in front of me, she waved the lacy, white dress that used to be Madelaine's.

"Does it fit?" I asked. Forgetting my bad leg, I jumped up, then had to lean against the dressing table until the pain went away.

78

Joyce didn't seem to notice, but Helen raised an eyebrow at me.

Frowning, I shook my head at her, signaling her to keep quiet. "Does it fit?" I asked Joyce. "Did the wardrobe mistress let out the waist? I mean, otherwise, how will I ever get into the thing?"

Joyce laughed. "Calm down. She took your measurements from the green costume. This one should fit perfectly. Raise your arms."

I did and she guided the costume over my head. I smoothed my hands down the slippery fabric. Then, putting as little weight as possible on my hurt leg, I pivoted in front of the mirror. The skirt floated out and swished around my legs. So pretty!

A couple of the girls whistled.

"A ballerina at the age of eleven," Helen said.

"I am not!" I said. My face burning, I darted a glance at Madelaine's reflection in the mirror. She crouched at the second dressing table. For an instant her face tilted toward mine. We stared into each other's eyes. Hers were wide and blue, glassy like the Bye-lo doll's. Glassy with tears? Hunching my shoulders, I dropped onto my rickety chair.

"That's right, Cam," Joyce said, "settle down so I can do your makeup."

When she had finished, she cocked her head to one side and studied me. "Let's do something about your hair."

She unbraided it, combed her fingers through the kinky strands, and fluffed them out. "Glorious!" she said, backing away to admire her work. "Bright and crinkly. Now you look like a half-pint Maggie Adams. But come on, kids, let's get this show on the road. All of you except Cam are to wait down here with Claire's mother. And you, doll, come upstairs with me for your first scene."

My heart did a flip-flop. The only scene which I had actually rehearsed as Beauty's Little Sister was the Vision Scene. In all the others I had only watched Madelaine and

79

my brother. But tonight I could follow him, couldn't I? Everything should be okay if only Luke didn't start something and Randall didn't stage any of his scary, awful jokes. A shudder ran through me.

"Come on, I said, Cam," Joyce called from the foot of the stairs.

Trying not to limp, I followed her up the hard, cold steps and into the wings. Luke was already waiting, his eyes round, his mouth soft and puffy, his shoulders hunched.

When he spotted me, though, he straightened up. Grinning, he pointed to one of his yellow Post-it Notes. Stuck to the flat that divided the first and second wings, it said, "Cammy Smith danced here!"

Chapter Fourteen

Curtains for Cammy

Beyond the heavy folds of the curtain the orchestra had begun playing.

"We go on from here," Luke said, grabbing my hand and pulling me to the second wing. "And pay attention," he added, really bossy, but his hands were cold and his tongue kept wetting his lips. So he must be a little scared.

There was no doubt about my being scared. Inside my chest my heart racketed like a bowling ball. And my shivering wasn't caused entirely by the backstage drafts.

"We haven't even warmed up yet," I said.

"Never mind, Cam," Joyce said behind me. "Luke's role requires no dancing at all. And yours doesn't until the Vision Scene. You'll have plenty of time to warm your muscles before then."

"But I can't even remember what I do first," I wailed.

Joyce spread her fingers and fluffed out my hair. "Relax, doll. You look lovely. Just follow your brother." She smoothed the lace collar of his blue velvet suit. "You know what to do, don't you, Luke?"

" 'Course," he said, but his tongue circled his lips again. "I just wish that Maddy . . ."

81

Joyce interrupted. "Quick. There's your cue, kids. Here's your crutch, Luke. Onstage. Now." And she pushed us out into the blue glow. The heavy curtain dragged up. Blackness yawned out front like a huge open mouth. The only lights were the red exit signs gleaming here and there like animal eyes. Eerie!

Leaning on his crutch, Luke took my hand again. "Just stay beside me, and like I keep telling Maddy, you'll do okay," he whispered.

I pressed my lips together. He sounded so sure of himself, so confident. You'd think he'd been dancing five years instead of only five weeks. But his small paw felt as cold as mine.

Onstage blue dawn brightened into sunrise. The colors washed into each other. Inside my chest a bubble began swelling, a balloon of happiness. I had to dance. I would dance, hurt leg or not!

From the opposite wings Maggie came leaping. Her pale pink gown flowed around her legs. Her feet flickered in chains of quick *brisés* and small jumps. Following her stumped her stage father, a role performed by a dancer named Paul. He tottered like an old man.

Looping an arm around her waist, he gestured with the other.

"He's telling her he has to go away on a business trip," Luke whispered.

"I know the story!" I hissed.

"Now he's asking what she wants him to bring her," Luke said. "Like Dad did in the good old days before he quit his job. Remember?"

"Be quiet! We're not supposed to talk onstage," I said.

Drooping against her father, Maggie shook her head.

"Dumb girl says she doesn't want anything," Luke said. "Next he'll ask us what we want."

Our stage father shuffled closer.

"Watch how its done," Luke whispered and tapping his

crutch ahead of him, hobbled a few steps downstage. Stopping there, he spun his free hand in tight spirals. He beamed at Paul, at Maggie, at me, at the whole, entire audience. What a ham! But somehow in the shafts of make-believe sunlight, Luke was no longer Luke. He was Beauty's little lame brother.

"Did you see?" he asked, my own brother again, returning to my side. "Wasn't I terrific? I told Dad I wanted a spinning top."

I sniffed.

"Now you gesture to tell him to bring you a doll," he whispered as I slid forward. Smiling toward the black auditorium, I remembered how at rehearsals Madelaine had shaped a head and body, then rocked her arms as if she were cradling a baby. I did that now.

"Great, Cammy! You too, Luke," Maggie whispered.

She gave each of us a hug before flying off to dance with her father.

"Beauty's changed her mind," Luke whispered. "Now she's asking him for a rose. The stupid rose that causes all the trouble!" He elbowed me in the ribs. "Come on, we gotta leave."

We exited slowly, Luke hobbling, I trying to skim like Maggie, no matter how much my leg hurt.

Frowning, Joyce met us in the wings. "Did you hurt your foot or something, Cam?"

Luke tilted his chin and smirked at me. If the brat told . . . But he didn't. Not then.

"No, my feet are just fine, Joyce. Perfect," I said quickly, which was true. It wasn't my feet that hurt.

She continued frowning. "Are you quite sure? Because I thought you might be limping a little. Well, come on, then, back downstairs. You have to stay in your dressing rooms until you're needed again."

"How'd it go?" Helen asked when Joyce returned me to the whitewashed cavern in the basement.

"Okay."

"Beautifully," Joyce said. "Cam was great. And so, of course, was Luke." He stood in the doorway behind us, waving at Madelaine.

"Out," Joyce said and nudged him into the hall when she left.

I slumped onto the chair beside Helen.

"How did your leg hold up?" she asked.

"Fine. And I don't want to talk about it."

I leaned toward the mirror to brighten my lipstick. I repowdered my face and brushed my hair. Most of the lovely crinkles were gone. My hair hung around my shoulders nearly dead straight again.

"Ready, doll?" Joyce said at the door again in practically no time, it seemed to me. "I've just collected your brother."

"It's more goodbyes," he told me in the wings. "Now it's goodbye to both Dad and Beauty. He has to go to the Beast's castle. So does she. If she refuses, her dad will die. He got caught in the Beast's garden stealing that stupid rose."

"Quiet in the wings," snapped a voice behind us. It was Randall, wearing the horns and claws of the Beast. "I can't concentrate, can't get properly into my role with all this chatter, chatter, chatter."

I shrank away but Joyce said, "Oh, lighten up, Larry," and gave Luke and me each a little shove. "That's your cue, kids. Get going."

The greenish light was supposed to turn the stage into a garden. Tonight, though, it reminded me of the mossy pond in our backyard. Mom had been nagging Daddy to fill it in ever since the raccoons ate the goldfish. Trying to skip around the stage on my hurt leg was like struggling through the pond's thick, green slime, the breeding place for black water bugs and mosquitos.

"Cammy, what's hurting?" Maggie whispered when her back was to the audience.

I looked away. "Nothing."

"Her leg," Luke whispered.

"It does not!" I said.

"Cammy, when you exit, tell Joyce," Maggie said as she kissed me, her little sister, goodbye. Luke and I limped to the wings, Luke on purpose, me because I couldn't help it.

Joyce met us.

Luke poked me. "Go on. Tell her."

I poked him back. "Let me alone."

"She hurt her leg," he said.

Joyce frowned. "I noticed. How bad is it?"

"Not bad," I said.

"Real bad," Luke said.

I gave him a shove. "It is not, tattletale. You want me out and your precious Maddy back in!"

He widened his eyes at me. "Just don't want you crippled for life, Cameo Cammy!"

"Yeah. Sure," I said.

"Quiet!" Joyce snapped. "We have a ballet to put on! Cammy, can you or can't you do the *arabesques* in the Vision Scene?"

"Are you kidding?" Luke asked.

Joyce glared at him and put an arm around my shoulders. "You know, Cam, it's bad to dance with an injury. Bad for you. Bad for the ballet. So tell me the truth. Can you do the *arabesques*?"

A sob blocked my throat. I couldn't talk. I shook my head.

She sighed. "Then it's curtains for you tonight, doll. We'll have to put Madelaine back in the Vision Scene."

"Far out!" Luke said, then glancing at me, ducked his head.

85

Chapter Fifteen

No Boys Allowed

"Stop him!" Joyce yelled down the stairwell to Claire's mother, who was still guarding the basement corridor. "I told him to stay away from Madelaine."

Joyce clattered after Luke to the girls' dressing room. I came behind, step by painful step, clinging to the banister.

"Don't let him in there," Joyce said. "He'll only upset her. We have enough problems without that! I'll break the news to her gently."

But Luke dodged past everybody and dived into the dressing room.

Shrieks went up. "No boys allowed!" Some of the girls no longer thought my brother was as adorable as they had at first.

"But I gotta talk to Maddy," Luke growled, his voice almost as deep as Daddy's. It rolled along the whitewashed walls of the corridor, up the stairs past me, maybe even into the auditorium where Mom and Daddy were watching *Beauty and the Beast*. If they had managed to finish dinner and get to the theater, that is.

Seconds later when I hobbled into the dressing room Luke

stood in front of Madelaine as straight and still as a toy soldier from *Nutcracker*. I had expected he would be hopping from foot to foot, his arms and feet swinging like those of a marionette. She leaned back against the dressing table, supporting herself on the skinny, milky stems of her arms. Her blue eyes had paled almost to white the way the color of a balloon fades when it's blown up.

"Maddy, they're giving you your old part back," Luke said. "You'll get to do your super-duper *arabesques* and show everybody how great you are. Then they'll have to give you a super big scholarship next year."

I chewed my lips. He was *my* brother, for gosh sakes. Didn't he care that it was *my* scholarship he was rooting for her to get?

Madelaine's lashes fluttered. "I can't, Luke. You know I can't."

Joyce snatched Luke by the shoulder. "Out! Before you ruin everything!"

"Leggo. If you want Maddy to dance her old part, let me talk to her."

"Get going!" Joyce said. She pointed toward the door with a finger nearly as rigid as Mom's.

Luke backed away. "You'll be sorry. I could talk her into it, Randall or no Randall. And even with her mom out in front."

I chewed a crinkly lock of hair. Would he please just shut up and leave! Hurt leg or not, I absolutely had to dance the *pas de deux*. For one thing, I wanted my own mom to see how talented I was.

"Goodbye Luke!" Joyce said. After he had banged off down the hall, she straddled the chair next to Madelaine's and leaned her wide, round chin on its curved back.

"We need you in your old part, Madelaine. Cammy's injured."

I dropped onto my chair beside Helen. She eyed me through her thick lenses. "I knew it. I knew it."

87

I stuck out my chin. "I could dance it if they'd just let me. Besides, it would look dumb, a redheaded Little Sister in the first scenes, a blond in the Vision Scene."

"Only the Vision Scene, Madelaine," Joyce was saying. "The scene where you do such nice high *arabesques*."

Madelaine shook her head. "You said if I came tonight, I only had to dance Cammy's old part."

"Yes, doll, but this is an emergency. And don't worry about Randall. I'll talk to him."

Madelaine kept shaking her head. "He scares me. With him around, I'll make mistakes. And my mother's in the audience."

Joyce's usually low, calm voice sharpened. "But, Madelaine, you don't even dance while Randall's onstage. You only have to stand there and watch him. The *pas de deux* comes after his exit. So what's the big deal?"

Madelaine lifted her sharp, bony shoulders. "I'll know he's there, watching. I can't, Miss Mallory. Somebody else will have to dance it."

"Only you and Cammy know the *pas de deux*, Madelaine. And Cammy's hurt. She can't dance it."

"I can, too," I shouted across the room. "I know I can."

"And I know I can't," Madelaine said, twisting her thin, bluish fingers. "I'll spoil everything like I did before, like Mr. Randall knows I will this time. And my mother's out there in the darkness, waiting for me to panic like in New York, waiting to laugh and laugh."

A knock rattled the dressing room door. "May I come in?" Blikk Eriksen called. And in he came. Smiling, he raised an eyebrow at Joyce. "Everything is arranged? Costumes? Cast changes? Time is running short. Act Three is nearly over. There remains only the intermission, then the Vision Scene."

Silence in the dressing room. But from far away in

88

the auditorium came the faint tones of Beauty's theme music.

"Cammy's pulled a hamstring," Joyce said.

Every head in the room pivoted toward me, including Blikk Eriksen's. "Badly?" the man asked.

I hunched my shoulders. His quiet voice brought tears to my eyes. I blinked them away and shook my head.

"Good. Good," he said.

"It's not good, Blikk," Joyce said. "Cam's hurt too badly to dance the *pas de deux*. And Madelaine refuses to."

Madelaine let out a long, shaky sigh.

Blikk Eriksen peered into her white face, then faced Joyce and raised an eyebrow.

She shrugged. "We'll have to skip the *pas de deux* to-night. Maggie can turn it into a solo. Too bad, though," she added.

Blikk Eriksen patted her shoulder. "But the *pas de deux* is your creation. So fresh, so charming. The two sisters, adult and child, dancing together."

"But I can dance it, really I can," I said, thinking of the long, low *penchés* and the graceful, high *arabesques*. "I just won't make the *arabesques* very high."

Joyce shook her head. "No way."

Blikk Eriksen smiled gently. "You would only aggravate your injury, my dear. When we perform it later in the season, maybe you will be able to dance it then."

I bit my lips to keep from crying. That wouldn't be until way after the demonstration. And was only a maybe. I wanted to dance it now, on opening night.

Joyce marched to the door. "I'll catch Maggie and Randall when they come offstage and tell them about the change."

Minutes later Joyce was back, followed by Maggie who wore a shawl pulled tight over her pink costume. Behind them ambled Randall, the thick tail of his Beast costume swinging inches above the floor.

89

"This place is becoming a virtual Grand Central Station," Helen said.

"Whatever happened to the no boys in the girls' dressing room rule?" whispered Claire, sitting just beyond Helen.

"Which kid is the one Joyce says I scared the bejabbers out of?" Randall drawled. With horns jutting from his cap, he looked like pictures of the devil in some of Daddy's art books. His vivid blue gaze swept the room and landed on me. "Besides eagle-eyed Tomasina, that is," he added with a whinny.

I ducked my head. He'd ruin everything for me yet!

Joyce sighed. "Who haven't you scared the bejabbers out of, Larry baby?" she asked mimicking his western twang.

"Funny! Funny! Just point out the girl you want me to apologize to."

"At the next table," Joyce said. "Madelaine Bettencourt."

"Aha!" Randall flipped back his tail with his heel and pranced across the room. In front of Madelaine's rickety chair, he dropped to one knee and flattened a hand over his heart.

Madelaine drew away, swaying. I expected her to topple over backward, but she didn't.

"My deepest, sincerest apologies. I'll never frighten the bejabbers out of you again, Megan," Randall said.

"Her name's not Megan. It's Madelaine," barked a voice from the doorway.

"It's Luke! It's Luke!" several girls shrieked.

"Luke, get out of the girls' dressing room," I yelled.

"As if he were the only male here," Helen whispered, wobbling her caterpillar eyebrows at me.

"Well, I can't have him here, talking Madelaine into dancing the *pas de deux*," I muttered. "I have to dance it myself. I just have to."

Randall spun around and glared at Luke. "You again, sonny?"

Luke jutted his chin. "I came to talk to Maddy. And nobody's going to stop me." He dodged Randall's long hands that reached to grab him and skidded to a stop beside Madelaine.

"Are you okay, Maddy?"

"Of course, she's okay," Randall said, towering above her. "And since I promised not to tease her anymore, she's going to dance the *pas de deux*, aren't you, darlin'?"

Madelaine shivered. She shook her head.

"And why not, I'd like to know? Haven't I apologized? Haven't I proved I'm not so beastly, after all?" he asked with his whinny of a laugh.

I licked my braces. A not-so-beastly Beast, ha! Of course, he hadn't tattled on me. Not yet. Just kept threatening to by calling me Tomasina.

Madelaine wilted against the back of her chair. She chewed a fingernail. "I can't dance it."

"Rubbish," said Randall, turning away. He slapped his palms together. "I wash my hands of the whole matter. This is what comes of having kids in a ballet!"

After Randall marched out, Luke leaned close to Madelaine. His orangish head touched her straw-colored hair. "Listen, Maddy, you and me together, we can do it," he said in a whisper you could hear over the entire room. "We'll make it a super ballet."

She shook her head. "Not with this man—this Mr. Randall. And not with my mother out there."

"Forget them, Maddy. Just dance."

Madelaine slumped farther down on her chair. "I can't forget him. I can't forget either of them. I'd be so scared I'd mess up just like in New York. I'd run offstage and my mother would end up in the hospital again."

Helen and I eyed each other. "The hospital?" I muttered. "What in the world happened to her?"

"It wasn't your fault, Maddy," Luke continued in his

resounding whisper. "It wasn't. She was already sick. And this time you won't get scared and split because I'll be there. It'll be like at the rehearsals. You and me together. And if Randall tries anything, just look at me and I'll wink. Like this. Then everything'll be okay. Okay?"

A smile barely lifted the corners of Madelaine's mouth. "Okay. If you're sure."

"Hey, I'm sure. I'm sure."

I pressed my lips together. Luke was always sure!

Chapter Sixteen

Strangers Backstage

"We'll make an exception to the rules for you, doll," Joyce said. She put an arm around my shoulders and gave them a brisk squeeze. "You may watch the Vision Scene from the wings. But only because you're injured, poor baby, and can't dance."

Not only couldn't I dance Beauty's Little Sister opening night, I wasn't even allowed to perform my old skipping role. "For your own good!" Blikk Eriksen and Joyce both had said.

So unless I was super fabulous in the school demonstration come April and got to dance in the first row, goodbye scholarship next year. Maybe goodbye ballet!

In the wings beside me, Joyce sighed. "Thank heavens for a wardrobe mistress as clever as Emma. A miracle worker. One touch of a razor blade and she expands the Little Sister costume for you. One touch of a needle and she shrinks it back for Madelaine. Look, it fits her perfectly."

Madelaine danced perfectly, too. High *arabesques*. Swelling insteps. No sign of sickling. Straight knees. And tonight, even though her mom was supposed to be in the audience, Madelaine concentrated on her role. You'd have thought she really was saying goodbye forever to her big sister. A beam from the gels shone on real tears. And like Luke's, her thin big-eyed face turned and returned to Maggie.

Once, though, I thought the Paragon was about to blow it. Somehow she wound up on the wrong side of the stage. Randall twisted his mouth into a sneer and growled something I couldn't hear but Madelaine must have. She shot a scared glance at Luke. He winked as he had promised and she sort of shook herself and was okay again. She glided to center stage to join Beauty and stretched into an *arabesque* almost as gorgeous as Maggie's.

After the kids finished they all crowded offstage to wait in the wings for curtain calls. "So you get to see the end of the ballet," Joyce said, "in case you don't remember how the old fairy tale turns out."

It ended happily, of course. When Beauty kissed the Beast on the snout, his horns, tail, and furry animal tunic dropped away to reveal a tall, smiling prince, with a movie star profile. Their love duet strung together perfectly balanced *pirouettes*, one-armed lifts, and finally a breathtaking fish dive. The curtain thudded down. The applause and bravos roared out front.

"Now's your big moment, so get out there," Joyce said and herded the kids onstage for curtain calls. All except me, of course, with my pulled hamstring.

Sighing, I watched them until a gawk of a woman barged between me and the stage. Her sharp elbow rammed into my shoulder. On purpose? What was she doing backstage before the curtain calls even ended?

"That hurt!" I said, rubbing the spot which was sure to turn black and blue.

The woman didn't answer. Maybe she hadn't heard. Not looking at me, she pushed by, head jutted forward. Her bony arms dangled from shoulder straps as thin as spaghetti. She glittered in a narrow, black evening gown stuck all over with sequins. The glare from the stage showed up a network of lines around her eyes and dark grooves under them. She looked as tired as Mom used to after studying all night for an exam.

Had the woman come backstage this early because she knew one of the dancers? Or maybe she was somebody important. A member of the Board of Directors of the ballet company or something.

"There she is, George," the woman said. Her raspy voice made me edgy like when Daddy filed the corners of frames for his paintings.

I frowned into the lights. Which dancer was she pointing out? The glare dazzled my eyes. And when I glanced back at the strangers I could see nothing but dim shapes outlined with light.

"She's in the line of children, George. Don't you recognize your own daughter?"

"Our daughter, Caroline," he said gently.

"All right, ours," the woman said with another harsh laugh that gave me the shivers. "Does that delight you, George?"

"Easy does it, Caroline. Now that she has a good teacher, she danced beautifully, don't you think? She's worked hard to please you, to be what you want her to be. So try to be kind."

"Oh, kind!" the woman said with the same shrill, bitter laugh. "When she slumps like that? See that darling red-headed boy she has by the hand? Now, he's standing like a dancer! Like a little prince!"

I caught my breath. She meant Luke. Taking curtain calls, Helen held him by one hand, Madelaine by the other. And I knew that this Caroline woman wasn't Helen's mother. I'd seen Helen's plump, tired mom hundreds of times sprawled

95

on a sofa at the ballet school, waiting to drive Helen home. No, this woman had to be the Paragon's mother. Now that I thought about it, she and Madelaine did look somewhat alike. Same long, skinny bodies. Same straw-colored permanents. Same narrow faces.

But their eyes, although the identical faded blue, were very different. The Paragon's were scared but lively, always looking around. Her mother's were like shallow pools left on rocks by the last high tide. Sometimes Daddy included one in a watercolor. No snails or starfish or sea anemones had yet had time to grow. Nothing filled them but clear salt water above a pebbly bottom. That was how empty this woman's eyes looked.

"George, I've got to get out of here," Madelaine's mother said. "It's so crowded. So stuffy. The sweat. The rosin. The grease paint. The stifling perfume. It's crushing me. It brings back that awful night in New York when I found out the truth: she'll never be a ballerina. Oh, get me out of here."

"We'll let her know we're here first, Caroline," the man said quietly. "And that this time you liked her dancing."

The woman's laugh filled the wings again. "But I didn't, George. It's the same as last time," she said, clutching her ears. "The noise. The smells. The blazing lights."

The woman swerved past me and wrapped both arms around one belonging to a dumpy, thin-nosed man. "Oh please, George, just get me out of here. I'll promise anything. I'll be kind to Madelaine. I'll tell her I liked her dancing."

"Tell her now, Caroline. Here she comes."

Madelaine came into the wings still holding Luke's hand. She dropped it when she saw her mom and dad.

The man hugged her. "You were wonderful, sweetheart, wasn't she, Caroline?"

96

"Yes. Yes. Now can we go, George?"

Luke thrust out his chin. "Maddy was terrific!"

If Madelaine heard him, she didn't let on. Her eyes fixed on her mother. Her frightening mom! No wonder she had been afraid of her coming. I would have been, too. And she wasn't even my mother!

"Mama, are you okay?" Madelaine asked.

"Yes. No," the woman snapped. "This place is closing in on me."

She shut her eyes and clutched her hands over her ears. "Come on, George. Just come on," she said and skittered through the wings and out the stage door.

The man hung back but his eyes reached after his wife. "Don't worry, Madelaine sweetheart. She'll be all right. As soon as we get home I'll check with the doctor. We'll wait for you in the car. But hurry."

As he turned to follow his wife, the working lights blazed on.

Until then he had been as much a stranger to me as the woman. Maybe I should have recognized him sooner. That thin-nosed profile. But he wasn't wearing the green cap with the visor. And his face wasn't framed in the window of Madelaine's white Mercedes.

"For gosh sakes, he's your chauffeur!" I exclaimed to Madelaine, following her and Luke toward the basement stairs. "Your father's your chauffeur. Your chauffeur's your father!"

"You got it," Luke said.

Madelaine ducked her head and nodded. Her eyes shone in the working lights. "He got the job after we moved out here. We came on account of Mama had been in and out of hospitals back there even before I blew it in *Nutcracker*. Long before," she said, her voice a thin wire unwinding and unwinding.

"Daddy heard about this hospital in San Francisco. We

97

had to sell our car back there along with almost everything else. But out here we have rooms above his boss's garage and Daddy gets to use the Mercedes to drive me to ballet and to visit Mom in the hospital. Only now, of course, she's home.''

Licking my braces, I hunched my shoulders. Madelaine ran ahead of us and down the basement stairs. My mind flooded with new and confusing thoughts. But one thing was for sure—Madelaine needed a scholarship as much as I did.

Chapter Seventeen

Move Over, Baryshnikov!

"You were terrific, bunny," Mom said, rushing backstage and grabbing Luke in a big hug. "So were you, Cammy," she added. "But you gave me the impression that you had a much bigger role."

I stuck out my chin. "I did. I did have a bigger part, but . . ." I broke off, too tired and discouraged to go into the whole, awful story. But at least she didn't start in on me with her reality nonsense about accepting things the way they are. The lecture always ended up the same: "If you don't have enough talent to become a professional dancer, it's time you stopped wasting time and money taking ballet lessons."

Behind Mom's shoulder, Daddy winked at me. "We loved every single instant you were on stage, Honey Bunch. Much more time up there and you'd have stolen the show from the star ballerina."

Grinning, he angled one arm above his head and touched a mottled-green forefinger to his balding crown.

"Oh, Daddy! Don't tease me," I said, a tear sliding down

99

one cheek. "Not tonight. And I could never, ever steal the show from Maggie Adams. Besides, I wouldn't want to. I'm not a scene-stealer like Luke."

But, lying in bed that night, an ice pack on my thigh, I got to thinking about his performance. Somehow, onstage he had changed from a brat into Beauty's sweet little brother. While he was saying goodbye to her, his face had followed Beauty everywhere—"like a sunflower follows the sun," the review in the *Chronicle* claimed the next morning.

The newspaper lay open on the kitchen table when I hobbled down to breakfast. Somebody, probably Mom, had circled the article with a red felt tip pen. The story discussed the freshness of Blikk Eriksen's choreography, mentioned Maggie's "lyricism and technical excellence," and reported that Randall "had lived up to his reputation as a fine *danseur noble*." Madelaine and the rest of us weren't mentioned, but students seldom were. That's why the comments about Luke were so surprising.

"Luke Smith, although only eight years old, shows amazing concentration, stage presence and precocious acting ability. He turned in a touching and convincing performance. By merely lifting his head he conveyed the sadness he felt at the loss of his sister. His face followed her like a sunflower follows the sun. Unfortunately, his was not a dancing role. But, if young Luke Smith dances as superbly as he acts, move over, Baryshnikov!"

Scowling, I poured myself a bowl of cereal and drowned it with milk. If Luke read that his head would swell to the size of a soccer ball. I slapped the review face down on the table so that he wouldn't see it.

He didn't, but people at school did, including Croaker. During the afternoon recess, when grades one through three went home, kids began charging past where I sat sideways on a bench, my hurt leg propped straight in front of me. More and more of them rushed by, crossed the blacktop, and ended up swelling into a mob that was gathering at the edge of the soccer field.

100

Up went the shout, "Fight! Fight!"

I hobbled to the fringe of the noisy crowd. I craned to see what was going on in the middle. Short for a sixth grader, I couldn't see over the bobbing heads and shoulders. And with my sore leg, I wasn't able to gain height by jumping. No mistaking Croaker's voice, though. It rasped from the very center of the hurricane.

"Here's the little sunflower, hisself! Like the newspaper said. Wimpy! Wimpy! Wimpy!"

I clenched my fists. That bully Croaker! He was a fourth grader, a whole year older than Luke. But who'd have thought the dummy could read well enough to sound out even the comics, let alone a ballet review!

"Nothing wimpy about ballet!" came Luke's shout also from the middle of the crowd.

"Is so. And that's what you are, Luke. Wimpy!"

"Take that back, Croaker."

"Try and make me, you wimp!"

A chorus of shouts followed. "You tell him, Croaker!" "Let him have it good!"

My hands curled into fists. Luke's friends must have gone right home when his class let out or been kept after school. Hadn't anybody waited around to stand up for my brother? Was he taking on Croaker's entire fourth grade gang?

I twisted past the kids at the edge of the crowd. I jabbed my elbows into some, my knees into others. "Let me by! Move! Out of my way!"

"Sock the wimp in the kisser!" someone yipped.

I pawed on through the mob. "I'm coming, Luke!"

"Yay, Croaker!" a kid cheered. "Give it to the little sunflower!"

"Let me through," I shouted, darting through an opening.

Then came the smash of flesh on flesh. Whose on whose? Had Croaker hit Luke, or the reverse?

Shoving between more kids, I yelled, "Hang in there, Luke. I'll be with you in a minute!"

Finally, there they stood. Croaker, a whole head taller, weaving his loaf-sized fists in front of my brother's nose. Luke, his red hair blazing in the sunlight, dodged and danced while darting his fists at Croaker. Then Luke connected. Blood, thick and red as spaghetti sauce, gushed from Croaker's nose and down his 49ers T-shirt. He staggered, one hand clutching his nose.

"Good going, Luke!" I shouted.

Luke, his hands still rolled into fists, didn't look my way. Listing from one foot to the other, he watched Croaker with the kind of concentration the ballet reviewer had been talking about.

A good thing, too. For suddenly Croaker lunged. His fist caught the corner of my brother's left eye. Split it. Blood spilled down Luke's cheek. Croaker started for him again but I rushed in.

"Let him alone, you big bully," I shrieked and yanked him away from my brother.

I beat my fists against Croaker's shoulder. It gave like rubber. "You big ox," I screamed. "Why don't you pick on somebody your own size!"

"Watch it!" someone yelled from the edge of the crowd. "Here comes a teacher!"

Others took up the chant. "Teacher! Teacher!"

A regular battalion of them marched onto the battlefield. One grabbed me away from Croaker. "For heaven's sake, Cammy, what got into you?" It was the librarian who always saved the new ballet books for me.

A janitor dragged Luke and Croaker apart. They stood, scowling at each other, panting, bleeding, arms hanging.

"The three of you, to the principal's office," a teacher ordered and a couple of them shooed us in front of them over the blacktop. In the office we backed onto wooden armchairs way too big even for Croaker. My Nikes just touched the gray carpet and Luke's dangled above it in mid-air.

Across the room from us, the principal sat behind her neat

desk and made a tent of her thin hands. Her mouth curled down like the sad faces Luke's teacher draws on my brother's math and spelling papers.

"All right, what's this all about?"

Croaker and Luke glowered at their shoes. Blood still oozed down their faces but it was turning rusty brown on the fronts of their T-shirts.

Our school didn't have a nurse so the principal passed them a box of Kleenex as if it were a plate of chocolate chip cookies. They each took one. Next came ice packs. The school secretary brought them in from the freezer top of the refrigerator in the teachers' room. Croaker held his to his nose, which had already swollen to the size and color of a red apple. The left side of Luke's face looked like the piece of steak Mom put on his eye after the last fight he got into.

"Cammy, suppose you tell us what happened," the principal said.

I scowled at Croaker. "He started it. He was teasing Luke about something in the newspaper."

"And what was that?" she asked.

"A review he read about a ballet Luke was in."

"I didn't read it," the Croaker said. "I wouldn't never read nothing as wimpy as that."

"Couldn't read it, you mean," I said.

Luke chortled. "Good one, Cam!"

"Shut up," Croaker snarled.

The principal's ruler rapped her desk top. "Quiet! That's quite enough of that! If you didn't read it, how did you know what the review said, Duane?"

Duane is Croaker's wimpy real name.

Croaker slid his spine down the chairback until he was resting on his neck.

"Sit up straight, Duane," the principal snapped. "And answer my question, please."

"The teacher read it right after lunch," Croaker said. "One of the kids who goes home to eat brought it. The

103

teacher said someone in our school had done something wonderful! Yeah. Sure. Something wimpy!"

Luke leaped to his feet. "Nothing wimpy about the bloody nose I gave you, Croaker Roaker!"

"Luke, sit down," the principal said. "So Duane teased Luke about being in the ballet and they started fighting. But how did you become involved, Cammy? I noticed you were limping."

"That didn't happen then . . ." I began but Croaker interrupted.

"She had to come save her wimpy ballet dancer brother."

Luke was out of his chair, reaching for Croaker. "She did not! But she got you good, didn't she?"

Then Croaker muttered something. The principal banged her ruler.

"Watch your language, Duane!" she said. "And you sit down, Luke!" Then she added, "Your teacher was right, Duane, to share Luke's achievement with your class. We all should be proud of him. But not of his fighting. Not of any of your fighting. You all know the rules. Absolutely no fighting at school for any reason whatsoever."

"I just came in to help out my brother!" I cried.

"Nevertheless, Cammy, you were fighting. So every day next week you, Luke, and Duane will remain after school."

"But Luke and I, we have ballet lessons after school," I cried. "And I've got final rehearsals for the demonstration at the school. We get our stage positions assigned next week."

"Not next week you don't," said the principal. "Next week you will be staying after school every single day, paying the consequences for fighting."

104

Chapter Eighteen

Front Row, Center

When Mom came in the front door that night, she jammed her grocery sacks on the sofa and collapsed beside them. "Your father phoned me not to bother picking you up from ballet. You wouldn't be there, he said. He also left a message with the secretary at the ballet school, saying you won't be in class all next week. Another fight, I understand. Both of you this time."

I stuck out my lower lip. "I had to help Luke, didn't I? It's just not fair that I can't go to ballet."

Mom shrugged. "Those are the consequences, my girl!"

Daddy clacked his paintbrush against the sides of his rinsing jar. "Let the consequences fit the crime, tra la," he sang.

"But Mom," I wailed, "what did the secretary say? Did she say I can still be in the demonstration?"

"She just took the message," Mom said.

Luke raced in from the kitchen with Foxy dancing around his legs. "You shoulda seen the blood gushing from Croaker's nose."

"Fortunately, I didn't have the pleasure," Mom said. "Now I'd better hear your version before Betsy calls with hers."

We hurried to tell Mom about the fight, me blurting the facts, Luke the gory details. "And that's when I let him have it in the snozzle," he finished just as the phone rang in the kitchen.

"That will be Betsy," Mom said and, gathering up the groceries, while the phone rang and rang, off she went. Foxy and Luke followed, one barking, the other yakking.

"Don't let Betsy give you a lot of dumb ideas," Luke said. "Like the time I said the F-word and you made me stand on the porch and yell it ten times into the neighbors' backyards."

The swinging kitchen door flopped back and forth behind them and the phone stopped ringing. But it wasn't Betsy on the phone. "It's your friend Helen," Mom called. "She probably wants to know why you didn't show up at the ballet class today."

I ran my tongue over my braces. Helen'd probably know if Madame had placed me first row, center, or if she planned to cut me out of the demonstration entirely.

"The most awful thing's happened," Helen said, not even saying hello. My stomach must have dropped a foot. Here came the bad news. "Cam, Mom gave me this choice. At least, she calls it a choice. Either quit ballet now and take a trip to Disneyland. Or quit ballet at the end of the term and not go to Disneyland."

I drew in my breath. "Some choice!" I said, knowing that now I couldn't possibly ask Helen about the demonstration and pile my troubles on top of hers. "How come your mother's making you quit?"

Helen's words came over the phone all blubbery. "The ballet school phoned Mom this morning and said I hadn't made enough progress this year so they've decided to drop me out of the professional division at the end of the term. Mom told me if I quit now, she'd take me to Disneyland with the money she'd save on tuition."

"What are you going to do?" I asked.

"Quit now. I mean, no more ballet no matter what. At least this way I get to go to Disneyland. That's why I wasn't in class today."

I chewed on my braid. So Helen wouldn't have the latest news about the demonstration.

"What'll I do without you, Helen?" I asked. "Who'll I talk to?"

After we hung up, I raced to the living room and clung to Daddy's prickly sweater. "Oh, Daddy, Daddy, everything's so awful. Helen's quitting ballet. The demonstration takes place the day after I get back. And if they don't let me be in it, I'll just die. They probably won't give me even half a scholarship."

"Well, Honey Bunch, don't worry about things before they happen." And, humming *Happy Days*, he touched the back of his hand to his painting to find out if it was dry.

That was when I got a look at the watercolor taped to his table: a dancer caught in banners of red and white paint.

"You didn't tell me you were painting Maggie Adams, Daddy."

He grinned. "Do I have to tell you everything?"

"And she's in the costume for *Beauty*. Did you copy it from her photograph in the souvenir program?"

"Nope. I sketched while she was dancing. People must have thought I was crazy, drawing away there in the dark. I used pastels so I'd remember the colors. See."

He handed me two raggedy sheets of thin paper torn from his sketchpad. Pink, red, and white streamers swirled around a dancer inside roughly outlined rectangles.

"They're positively beautiful!" I said. "Even better than the painting because Maggie's alive and moving in them. *Pirouetting*. Jumping."

He gave a shy laugh and a little shrug. "I don't know about their being better. You may have them, though, if you like."

"Oh, thank you, thank you," I said, hugging him. "Can I give them to Maggie?"

107

"I don't see why not."

"Oh, fabulous! I'll take them to her tomorrow."

Then my breath caught. I wouldn't be going to ballet tomorrow. I wouldn't be going for a whole, entire week. So I wouldn't be seeing Maggie.

Daddy came to my rescue, though. The next afternoon when I finally got home from staying after school, he sprayed fixative on the sketches and helped me put them in a bubble-lined envelope. I mailed them to Maggie the next day.

Two other good things happened that week. Well, the first was only half good. When I couldn't stand the suspense any longer, I phoned the ballet school and talked to Madame Harper. "Of course, you can still be in the demonstration, my darling, but what row you'll be in depends on how the final rehearsals go. And how well you're dancing after missing a week of classes." I groaned.

The completely good thing was a note from Maggie. Even before opening the envelope, I smelled her rose perfume. On the front of the note paper a pair of Degas dancers did *pliés*. On the inside Maggie's spidery handwriting slanted across the page. "Dear Cammy, what a lovely surprise. And what lively drawings. I just love them. Hang in there, Honey. See you when you return."

I didn't return until five more days, including the weekend, had dragged by. But at least not dancing gave my leg a chance to heal. It was okay again by the time the week of staying after school ended on Friday. The instant our classes let out that afternoon, Luke and I raced to catch the bus to the train depot.

When we arrived at ballet headquarters, rehearsal bedlam flowed out of the classrooms and down the stairs. Strains of Chopin, Mozart, and Prokofiev tangled with the shouts of teachers, "*Crosé devant,* young ladies!" "Keep the tempo, children!"

"Hey, I just remembered tomorrow's that big show," Luke yelled above all the noise.

"Yes, and I'm going to dance first row, center," I said, trying to sound positive. If I sounded sure enough, maybe I would.

"No, you're not. Maddy is," Luke said.

I frowned. "How do you know? You haven't been here for a week either."

"Telephone, what did you think?" he asked. "And next year I'm going to dance front row, center, too."

"If you're still taking ballet," I said. "And if you're in a regular class by then. Only kids from regular classes get to dance in the demonstration. So far you're not in any class at all."

"I am so. I'm in a class by myself. In Mr. E's. Now I've got to go change."

Before I could retort, he shoved past me, off to the men's dressing room to pull on regulation practice clothes. After finding out that Baryshnikov and the men in the company worked in them, my brother no longer considered tights wimpy.

Changing into practice clothes, too, I had this feeling that something important was missing from the girls' dressing room. Helen! Her round eyes. Her caterpillar eyebrows. Her big words. Even her wheezing. And upstairs in the classroom, there was no Helen to joke about the ribbon around the Paragon's topknot—yellow this time—or about Madelaine as usual grabbing the best place at the *barre*. I sighed. Now I knew why the Paragon did these things. I found a space and began bending my knees in *pliés*.

Madame Harper hobbled in. Should I go ask her now if I was at least in the first row of our class dance? But before I could, she lowered herself onto her creaking chair and clapped her hands for class to begin. "Places, please. *Demi-pliés.*"

After *barre* exercises we worked in the center on *développés*. In front of me Madelaine did her usual ear-nudging extentions. I stuck out my chin and sent my leg as high as possible.

"No, Cammy, don't strain for height," the teacher called.

"Especially not on your first day back. Just keep your hip down and work conservatively."

Next came *pirouettes* from fourth position. Everybody did single turns except Madelaine. She spun doubles—even one triple. Trying for a double, I stumbled off the ending.

"Lift from the waist, Cammy," Madame said. "And do only singles. But do them perfectly."

I pulled up, rose on half toe, and turned a slow, balanced *pirouette*.

"Good," the teacher called. "Wonderful."

Happiness bloomed inside me. Praise from Madame Harper! Maybe Luke was wrong and I'd get the first row, center position after all.

"All right, my darlings," the teacher said, glancing at her watch. "It's time for us to go down the hall to rehearse in the little theater. Line up and follow me."

The little theater was at the end of the corridor, really just two classrooms, usually separated by an accordian-pleated divider. Today, with the flexible wall pushed open, the two studios were one. The room that served as a stage rose three steps above the one where the audience would sit on creaking, folding chairs, the kind Daddy called my-aching-back chairs.

We all followed Madame onto the stage. "Places, please," she said.

I stood nibbling my lower lip. The other kids formed three rows of five dancers each. The first row, the one in front, had only four.

Madame Harper pointed to a space between Madelaine and Claire. "Cammy, we saved that spot for you."

Claire stood at the end of the row, me next to her. That put Madelaine in the very center, just as Luke had said. But I'd still be seen, wouldn't I? And have a chance for a scholarship?

"Thank you, Madame," I said and sped to my place.

Madelaine slid her eyes in my direction. "Hi, Cammy." A faint smile curled her lips. She giggled. "Not even a black

110

eye. How is Luke's eye?'' I frowned. Had my brother told her absolutely everything about the fight?

Our teacher nodded to the pianist. And to the familiar Chopin étude we skimmed through our variation. When it ended, Madame sat eyeing us and frowning. I pressed my lips together. What had we done wrong? Or was it only me after not taking class for a whole week? Madame's chair squawked. Struggling out of it, she limped toward us.

"It needs something. More interest. A focus.''

She paced in front of us, her earrings swinging, her steps lurching and uneven, her long taffeta skirt whispering. Back and forth. Back and forth. Suddenly she stopped in front of Madelaine.

"You don't blend in with the little girls.''

Madelaine sucked in her lips. She twisted her thin fingers and pulled at her yellow ribbon. "Sorry,'' she whispered.

"It's nothing to be sorry about, my darling. It's just that your technique is more advanced and your body is stretching out into a young woman's.''

Grasping Madelaine's hands, she pulled her out of line.

"You're to do your double *pirouettes* and high extensions out here in front of everybody. By yourself. Alone. Do you understand?''

Her cheeks turning pink, Madelaine nodded. "Yes, Madame. Thank you, Madame.'' Then the Paragon's glance swung to me. Her lips formed the word "sorry'' again. I chewed my lips. My insides churned. Oh, sure! Sorry!

Now, like the advanced classes, ours would have a soloist. A star. And it wasn't me. It was Madelaine.

Chapter Nineteen

Class Stardom

"You'd better change into whatever you're going to wear to dance in tonight," Mom called late the next afternoon. It was time to leave for the demonstration. The demonstration that starred Miss Madelaine Bettencourt, not Cammy Smith. "There will be a slight delay while your father tinkers with Old Faithful's insides—something to do with the water pump."

"But I'm supposed to be at the school two hours early to warm up and things," I wailed.

"Complain to your father. I'm not the one who didn't come to a good stopping place."

I put on my so-called costume, the same leotards and tights and smudged pink technique shoes I wore in class, lesson after lesson after lesson. Only the advanced students got to dance in real costumes tonight.

And it proved a good thing I already had on my practice clothes when we finally got to the school. By then there was barely enough time to strip off my sweater and skirt, warm up, and make up before we had to go onstage.

Mom and Daddy dropped me and Luke at the front door, then drove away to look for a parking place. Luke, who of course wasn't in the demonstration, slouched after me into the foyer, hands in the pockets of his new cords. His job was to save three folding chairs in the classroom where the audience would sit tonight. Seats weren't reserved but were on a first-come basis.

"Window on the Future!" he muttered. "Don't they know that Lukenikov is the future?"

I loped upstairs to the classroom that tonight had been turned into a dressing room for our class. Already seated along the makeshift picnic tables that had been dragged upstairs from the school patio, the other girls were peering at themselves in small propped-up mirrors and smearing on make up. Wreaths of fake pink flowers ringed their topknots.

On a chair near the door crouched our teacher in a long black dress. Shiny jet earrings jangled at her ears. An orange bird of paradise flower sat on her shoulder.

"The late Miss Smith," she snapped. Her eyes, black as her earrings, snapped, too. "We're third on the program and everyone has already warmed up except you."

Stabbing a black felt tip at the sheet of paper on her clipboard, Madame Harper checked my name off the class list.

I dropped onto the only unoccupied place, a spot on the bench at the very end of the last picnic table. Helen wasn't here anymore to save me a seat.

Down the table from me Madelaine bent toward one of the small mirrors. Glancing at her, I met her eyes. They were as shadowed underneath as her mother's had been backstage the night *Beauty* opened.

"You came, finally," she whispered.

I started to explain about Daddy and his watercolor washes and Old Faithful's water pump but she turned to Madame. "Now Cammy's here and can take my place. I have to go home. My mother is—my mother needs me."

I slid another look at Madelaine. Her face seemed thinner than ever. White tissue paper over tiny, sharp bones. She wanted me to dance in her place. Out in front of the rest of the class. A solo. Me, Cammy Smith!

113

"You can go home soon enough, my darling," Madame said. "As soon as our class finishes dancing. And you, Cammy, never mind the make up. Just warm your muscles. Hold on to the dressing table. No, don't strangle it, child! Do a thorough *barre*."

I rounded my shoulders. My heart racqueted around my chest. A thorough *barre*! Did the teacher want to make sure that I was really warmed up so that if Madelaine wouldn't dance, I could? I bent my knees in *pliés*.

The dressing room door banged open and in zoomed Joyce. She closed it and sagged against it. Her face, that always smiled so easily, wasn't smiling.

"Madelaine, your father's down in the foyer. Go quickly."

The Paragon shot up from her chair. "Is my mother with him?"

Joyce shook her head. "Your father's alone and wondered if your mother maybe was here. I told him no and he said for you to come right away."

Madelaine grabbed her coat, didn't even bother to drape it over her practice clothes. She flashed out of the room.

I licked my braces. What could be wrong with her mother? I thought about the skinny woman who had barged backstage just as *Beauty* ended. Empty eyes. Shrill laugh. Recalling the laugh, I shuddered.

The dressing room was quiet, waiting for Madelaine to return or not to return. Joyce, usually so matter of fact, so used to running things, nibbled a thumbnail.

Finally footsteps bounded along the hall. But instead of Madelaine, Luke plunged into the room. Why wasn't he saving seats for Mom and Daddy?

"Stay out!" the girls cried.

Not looking at them, Luke marched to Joyce and Madame Harper. "I got a message from Maddy. She won't be dancing tonight."

I froze in the middle of a *frappé*. Would I replace her?

"Why won't she be dancing?" chorused the girls. "How come? And at the very last minute!"

Luke scowled at them, then left.

"All right, everybody," Joyce said, "pull yourselves together. It's almost curtain time."

"Then Madelaine's definitely not dancing?" Madame Harper asked.

"Definitely not, Natalie. You'll have to use her understudy."

My face burned. A shiver ran through me. Chills and fever. Was I coming down with the flu? The understudy had to be me!

"There is no understudy," Madame said. She struggled out of her chair and paced behind our chairs. Step-lurch. Step-lurch. "Too bad. The child provided such a wonderful focal point out there in front. No one else in this class stands out like that."

I caught my lower lip between my teeth. What about me? I wanted to shout. Maybe my extensions weren't ear-high yet and my *pirouettes* were still only singles, but DBM—the days before Madelaine—I had been the best in the class.

Madame Harper made another pass through the room before she faced us.

"Only four girls in row one and five in the others should give the variation some focus. Anyway, we'll dance it as originally planned."

Chapter Twenty

The Chalked "X"

"Quiet," Madame snapped. "Walk like dancers."

She marched us from our makeshift dressing room and lined us up in the hall outside the studio which would be our stage tonight. From down the corridor came the shufflings and voices of the audience gathering in the adjoining classroom. But from us there wasn't a sound except the rasp of our soft leather ballet shoes on the linoleum and a giggle now and then. I slouched along, shoulders sagging. My heart, too. Why couldn't I be the star in Madelaine's place?

I touched my topknot to make sure my slippery braid hadn't skidded free of its bobby pins. I hummed *Happy Days*, hoping that without Madelaine in *Window* I'd have a better chance at a scholarship.

When we reached the studio door the little kids in Classes One-A and One-B hunched together, buzzing like bumblebees. Which they also resembled with their round bodies stuffed into black leotards. Mostly nine-year-olds, they were the babies in the school's professional division.

After they scurried onstage, one remained behind. Luke! He had stood so still in their midst that I hadn't seen him even though, unlike the others, he wasn't wearing practice clothes. He had on his new cords and a sports shirt.

"How come you're out in the hall?" I muttered. I grabbed him and pulled him towards the other classroom where I hoped Daddy and Mom had managed to find a seat even without my brother's help. "Only the kids in the demonstration are supposed to be here."

He stuck out his chin at me. "Leggo," he said, yanking himself free. "I had to help Maddy, didn't I?"

"So where is she?"

"Looking for her mom."

"Maybe her mother's in the audience expecting to see Madelaine dance."

"She isn't. We've already checked three times."

"Then maybe she's around here someplace. In an empty classroom. In a doorway," I said, glancing over my shoulder toward the shadows at the end of the hall. A quaver shook me.

"She's not down there, dummy, if that's why you're looking so scared."

I sniffed. "Who's scared?" I asked, remembering the woman's weird laugh. "How about where Madelaine lives? They checked there?"

" 'Course. But her mom's not there anymore. She was. She stayed, wouldn't go with Maddy and her dad when he drove Maddy to the demonstration. When he got back, her mom wasn't anywhere in their rooms."

"Maybe she went to the store or somewhere."

"Somewhere's about right. They've hunted everywhere, with me helping here. She's just plain lost."

Then Luke said it. I didn't. "Lost like those old ladies at the bus depot talked about. Only Maddy's mom's not a kid and won't get her picture on a milk carton."

I drew a sharp breath. At least this time it wasn't Luke I imagined lost somewhere out there in the foggy, dark city.

117

Suddenly a hand gripped my shoulder. A scream rose at the back of my throat. A voice ordered, "Hush, both of you!" It wasn't Madelaine's mother. It was Madame Harper. Her earrings flapped furiously. But I had never been so glad to see anybody in my life! "What's your brother doing here, Cammy? He's not in the demonstration. Shoo, little boy!"

Luke backed away and Madame continued barking at me. "Hear that music? That means we're next."

She guided me, none too gently, back to the line of familiar faces. All the kids from my class were there except Madelaine. And Helen, of course, with her wry half-smile and glint of glasses. I licked my braces. Well, I sure hoped she had a really great time at Disneyland!

The bee-shaped babies ahead of us on the program scrambled offstage and into the corridor. They giggled with excitement. A few of us giggled, too. Including me, mostly from nerves.

"Hush!" Madame Harper snapped. "Be quiet and follow me." She led us into the studio and onto the stage. Tonight a curtain of heavy cotton separated the two rooms instead of the accordion-pleated divider. "Places, everybody."

We scrambled into our lines and pressed our feet into tight fifth positions. I drew a quavery breath. Just ahead of me on the non-skid floor covering gleamed the chalked "X" where Madelaine should be standing. For a second I almost wished she were there to hide any terrible mistakes I might make.

Two girls from Class Seven opened the heavy curtain. The room where the audience sat was dim, but rows of faces shone ghost-pale in lights strung on makeshift flys above the stage section. Was the face of Madelaine's mother among them? And how about those of my parents?

A few coughs, the squawking of the folding chairs, and the crackling of paper programs drifted up to us. The tape deck blared the opening notes of our Chopin étude. Then, while

118

we waited through the bars of introduction, someone flashed across the stage in front of us. I stiffened but the person was much too short to be Madelaine. Or her mother. Whoever it was stopped on the white "X" directly in front of me and snapped his or her feet into an exact fifth position. Red hair flamed in the glare of the overhead lights.

I gasped. Luke! And in practice clothes. His own. Brand new. Shiny black technique shoes. Black, unfaded tights. And decorating the back of his white T-shirt, a red-brown rust stain shaped sort of like a sea horse. It had rubbed off our old clothes line which Mom was always trying to get Daddy to string with new, rust-proof wire.

Like me, Luke must have come here with his practice clothes under his street clothes. But when we left home this afternoon he couldn't possibly have known that Madelaine wouldn't be dancing tonight.

"Cammy, it's your idiot brother," Claire hissed beside me. "Get him out of here," somebody else whispered. "He'll ruin everything." Teetering at the edge of the stage, Madame Harper motioned furiously. "Boy, get off the stage!"

"Luke, you little creep," I growled, "what are you doing out here?"

What he was doing, of course, was stealing the show away from me, away from the entire class.

Luke ignored all of us. He didn't move. Just stood there like a carving of a dancer—like a little prince, Madelaine's mother had said—head up, chest out, legs pulled straight and strong, muscular for an eight-year-old's. They resulted from years of tree climbing, roof hopping, soccer playing, and general wild racing around.

Which he would continue doing tonight, no doubt, leaping off in every direction, invading our demonstration just as he had invaded our audition for *Beauty*.

"Luke, I'll get you for this," I muttered. No answer. I clenched my fists, wanting to push him offstage, but how could I in front of everybody?

The tape sounded our cue and we slid into the first *glissade*. So did Luke, without even looking back to follow what we were doing. It was as if he could see us in the kind of tiny rearview mirror bicyclists wear on their helmets. He danced all the steps we did at the exact same time we did them: the *glissades, développés, pas de bourrées, changements, assemblés*. He knew every one. How had he learned them?

Of course, he didn't bother pointing his toes or taking exact positions or turning out from the hips. Not Luke. He went for height. Incredible height! Especially his *changements*. His red locks flapping, he leaped three feet off the floor. Bravos followed.

I lifted my chin. The brat needn't think he could spoil everything for me. Pretending the clapping was all for me, I smiled over the top of his head. I pointed my toes and tried for precise positions and a good turn-out. I skimmed the *glissades*, bounced the *pas de bourrées*, soared into the *assemblés*. Soon the music lifted me, floated me. In the final *changements*, I flew off the floor, up, up, and changed my feet high in mid-air. I landed in the position we had started from—fifth. So did Luke. And, to my astonishment, he didn't add any fancy extra leaps, didn't skid to the brink of the orchestra pit, didn't ham up the ending by landing spectacularly on one knee.

Applause thundered. And bravos. Which were obviously for Luke because audiences shout bravos for boys, bravas for girls. Then a half dozen bravas roared for the rest of us. Hurrah! Luke hadn't stolen the whole show, after all.

During curtain calls, Luke surprised me again. He didn't dash forward to bow in front of us all, claiming the applause for himself like Randall did lots of times. No, Luke backed into line next to me. He flashed me a grin.

"How was I, Cammy Wammy?"

I gave a grunt. "How'd you know the steps?"

"Maddy taught me. Who else?" He smirked as our line,

120

including him, marched forward. We girls bobbed our heads and dropped our right knees in curtsies. Luke doubled over from the waist to make a simple bow. Again no corny Lukenikov flash!

When curtain calls ended, he trailed offstage with us, out into the hall and into a mob of kids waiting to go on. Across the corridor from us and near the door of our dressing room Madame Harper was signaling to us like crazy. She wanted us to come to her. But how could we get through this crowd? Claire was jammed against my right side, Luke against my left.

"Okay, Luke," I said. "What's the story?"

He smirked. "Story? What story are you talking about?"

I jabbed my elbow into his shoulder. "You planned it all along, didn't you?"

"Well, not all along. Not until after Maddy got promoted to class star."

"Star!" I growled, pressing my lips over my braces. "That was only yesterday. So how'd Madelaine have time to teach you the steps?"

"Easy! I've known them all along. Since rehearsals for *Beauty*. I got bored sitting around, not dancing. Not even in class. All Mr. E. gives me there are dumb exercises. The basics, he calls them. So Maddy taught me your demonstration dance. Then yesterday we decided I'd dance it with your class."

I sniffed. "We? You and Madelaine decided?"

He grinned. "Okay, I decided. But Maddy thought it was a great idea too." He sighed. "Only we didn't get to dance it like we planned. Together. In a duet, she called it. But when her mom disappeared tonight, I said I'd go ahead and dance it solo. Which was okay with Maddy."

Pouting, he hunched his shoulders. "Wish she'd danced it with me, though." Then he grinned. "But I did do you all a great big favor. Who do you think all that clapping, all those

121

bravos were for? Me! Hey, without Lukenikov the Great, the whole dance would have been one huge flop!''

Somebody laughed behind us. Joyce, who with Madame Harper had finally reached us through the mass of students. ''A slight exaggeration, kiddo, but you did provide a certain amount of, shall we say, pizzazz? Didn't you think so, Natalie?''

Madame laughed. ''Yes, indeed. Tossing red hair. Obviously delighted to be dancing. Also delighted with himself. I only wish that Madelaine had consulted me about her replacement.''

''She should have,'' said Blikk Eriksen, showing up behind Joyce. ''The cast and any cast changes should be entirely the prerogative of the choreographer.''

Then, not even glancing at Luke, the man flashed his smile at me. ''You danced very well tonight, Cammy my dear. Nice and light. Precise positions, too.''

My heart leaped. ''Oh, thanks . . .'' I began, my face burning with pleasure. But Blikk Eriksen turned to Luke. I chewed my braid which had slipped over my shoulder. Now would come all kinds of praise for my brother, just what the swellhead didn't need!

''And you, young man,'' Blikk Eriksen said, ''although your impetuous performance may have added interest to Class Two's simple little variation, you could have ruined a more complicated piece.''

Luke ducked his head. ''But I did all the steps right, Mr. E., exactly as Maddy showed me. I started right on the 'X.' Maddy said not to add anything extra—improvise, she called it—and I didn't.''

''That may be true, Luke,'' Blikk Eriksen said. ''But dashing in like that and dancing without permission indicates that you still have much to learn about discipline and responsibility.''

Luke drooped, shrank together sort of like a burned-down candle.

I licked my braces. "But Mr. Eriksen, Luke did do all the steps right. I mean, he minded what Madelaine said. He didn't go jumping around, making up his own crazy wild variations."

Luke stared at me. His mouth dropped open, soft and red. He stood up straight.

Blikk Eriksen smiled. His shimmery gray eyes turned almost silver. "Well, perhaps your brother is making some progress, after all, Cammy. And so are you!"

Chapter Twenty-one

Window on
the Future

Intermission was over by the time I had changed, combed my hair, and scrubbed off my makeup. The lights snapped off just as I slid onto one of the seats ribboned off out front for students from the demonstration. Seconds later Helen, of all people, plopped down on the folding chair next to mine. I grabbed her around the shoulders in a big hug.

"You came! Am I ever glad to see you!"

Helen's glasses flashed in the lights from the stage. "Likewise. You didn't really think I'd miss the demonstration, did you? And what a demonstration with that crazy sibling of yours stealing the show!"

I grunted. "Tell me about it!"

"Hush, my darlings," Madame Harper hissed from somewhere in front of us just as the second half of *Window* began. It included not only class exercises by the older students but solos by the really good ones.

Helen and most of the kids around us clapped and whistled for their favorites, especially for the pair dancing the final number on the program, a *pas de deux* from *Beauty*.

124

Madame Harper, sitting two rows ahead of us, turned her sleek, dark head, silhouetted now against the glow of the stage. "Quiet down back there. That includes you, Cammy!"

"But," I began, open-mouthed. I'd been applauding politely, not whistling or stamping like the others. Having seen Maggie Adams float through the *pas de deux* ruined seeing anybody else dance it.

The two students took their bows. Then Blikk Eriksen, all silvery in a light gray suit that matched his hair and eyes, bounded out in front of the curtain. I sank lower on my creaking chair. Here came what I had been both dreading and looking forward to: the announcement of the students who would receive scholarships next year. I just had to have one, a whole one, Mom had said, or no ballet come fall.

"Ladies and gentlemen," Blikk Eriksen began in his precise, unaccented English. "You have looked through a window into the future of ballet and seen some of tomorrow's dancers. Now to help a handful of them toward that future, we will award a few scholarships. I wish we had more to give, especially to some of our gifted younger pupils."

"So do we, huh, Helen?" I said. Then, frowning, I chewed my lower lip. For a minute I'd forgotten not only that Helen was no longer a candidate for a scholarship, she was no longer a ballet student.

"Unfortunately," Blikk Eriksen went on, frowning slightly and rubbing his hands together, "because of government cutbacks, changes in tax laws, etc., our funds are very limited this year. We believe that most of the scholarships should, therefore, go to talented, more advanced students. Year after year, they have worked hard to make progress, thus proving their ability and their serious intentions of becoming professional dancers."

I twisted my braid while he reeled off the names of older students, at least a dozen of them. Would there be a scholarship left for me?

"Now we come to our younger students," Blikk Eriksen

said. "First of all, we are awarding a full-tuition scholarship to encourage an unusually gifted youngster to pursue a career in ballet. His name did not appear on the program tonight but you must have noticed the lively young man dancing with Class Two. Luke Smith."

The auditorium exploded with applause and laughter. Three rows ahead of me, Luke jumped up and bowed. My face blazing, I slid my spine down the back of my chair. None of the older kids who had received scholarships had even waved a hand to let people know who they were or where they were sitting.

"Can you believe my brother?" I muttered to Helen. "Do you think he was the last to get a scholarship?"

Helen shook her head. "Blikk Eriksen said your brother was 'first of all.' So that means there'll be more."

I sighed. "Madelaine, then, even if she didn't dance tonight."

"I noticed," Helen said. "Did she chicken out again because of her mother?"

"No. Her mom's the reason, though. She's lost," I said with a shiver. "Madelaine and her dad are out looking for her."

Frowning, I thought of all the gray city streets and dirty little alleyways she could be wandering along, scared maybe, not knowing where to go.

"And now, ladies and gentlemen, our final scholarship," Blikk Eriksen said.

I pressed my cold hands together to try to stop their shaking. It had to be for either me or Madelaine, didn't it? Which would it be?

"Our final scholarship goes in an even split to a pair of talented young ladies in one of the lower classes."

Helen and I traded glances. "You!" she whispered.

I pushed my tongue along my braces. "Oh, I don't know. I don't know."

"One half is for a student who was unable to dance

126

tonight," he said, "because of an illness in her family. Madelaine Bettencourt."

Everybody applauded. Including me and Helen.

"The poor kid needs it," Helen said, "a sick mother and the chauffeur turning out to be her father. Sometimes people sure aren't what they seem at first."

I nodded. "Funny thing is, my brother knew it all along. I just hope the other half scholarship . . ."

Before I could say what I hoped, Blikk Eriksen said it for me. "The other half goes to Cammy Smith."

My heart cartwheeled. Helen and I shrieked and squeezed each other's hands.

"That's terrific," she said, but behind her glasses her eyes shone with tears. Tears of happiness for me? Or, despite her lumpy feet and hay fever, for dead dreams of her own? She had, after all, studied ballet for five years, one and three quarters of them here in this school's professional division. So, although she had never said so even once, she must have had the same dreams I had.

Suddenly a thought struck me like a kick in the stomach. If only half a scholarship didn't satisfy Mom, goodbye to my dreams, too.

Around us kids were applauding me. Crazy Luke leaped up and this time pumped his hands above his head like a winning boxer on TV. "That's Lukenikov's sister Cammy!" Everybody in the auditorium cracked up. I laughed, too. "When he gets over wanting to be a dancer—and he will, I'm sure he will—maybe he'll become a comedian," I said to Helen.

But she was no longer beside me. Looking toward the back of the room, I saw her plunging up the aisle with her mother and out the door. So Helen's tears hadn't been for my success, at least not entirely. Poor Helen! Tomorrow I'd phone her.

Sighing, I stared after her until my own mother, followed by Daddy, skirted through a tangle of folding chairs scattered

127

like the pieces of a jigsaw puzzle. Both of them hugged me. Mom first.

"Congratulations, Cammy. Seems you have some talent, after all."

"You bet you do, Honey Bunch! Lots of it."

"Thanks," I said, then waited for Mom to bring up the puny size of my scholarship. She didn't. Neither did Luke, who chugged up to us, grinning. "Lukenikov and sister about cleaned up! Maddy too."

Behind me a sweet, laughing voice said, "Cammy, Luke, you both were terrific. Congratulations!"

It was Maggie Adams. She patted Luke's rumpled red head and wrapped her arms around me.

"I didn't know you'd be here, Maggie," I said. "Larry Randall sure isn't, is he?" I asked, drawing in my breath and quickly scanning the crowd for his yellow head. It would be just like him to bring up the Tomasina bit tonight. Which he'd kept quiet about. So far.

Maggie laughed. "No, Larry never shows up at demonstrations. Or anything else having to do with children. But I wouldn't have missed it for the world. Doug wouldn't either," she added, smiling up at her tall, gorgeous husband.

Luke reached out and shook Doug's hand. "I'm Lukenikov, winner of the Super-Duper, Worldwide Easter Bunny Jumping Contest."

Everybody laughed except me. Enough was enough!

Then Maggie turned her beautiful smile on Daddy. "And you're the artist who did the lovely sketches of me."

Daddy's face grew pink. "Well, yes." How can Daddy be so shy with a son just the opposite?

"I really love them, Mr. Smith. I showed them to Blikk. He thinks they're great, too. In fact, he wonders if you'd let the company use them in promotion brochures. And maybe in next year's souvenir program, too."

Daddy's face went from pink to vermilion. "Well, I don't know."

"Of course, you know, Lloyd," Mom said. "He'll be delighted."

"Alice, they're only sketches."

"You'd be paid, of course," Maggie said. "I don't know how much. You'll have to talk to Blikk or the promotion manager."

I gave Daddy a big squeeze. "How great."

But he was frowning. He brushed his fingers through his thin hair. "About the sketches," he said. "I'd like the ballet company to use them, but I don't want money for them."

"For gosh sakes, Daddy, why not?"

Mom echoed my surprise.

"Because," Daddy said, "I'd like to exchange them for Cammy's ballet lessons, for the half that the scholarship doesn't cover. If I got paid for them, the money might go for something frivolous," he added, grinning at Mom, "like mortgage payments or food or new water pumps."

She grinned back. "Good point, Lloyd!"

I threw my arms around him again. "Oh, Daddy, you're the greatest!"

Maggie laughed. "I'm sure you can work out an agreement with Blikk. He's over there. Come on, I'll introduce you. And you, Cammy honey, I'll see you when we start rehearsing the sisters' roles in *Beauty* next month."

I started. "But what about Madelaine? Won't she be dancing Beauty's Little Sister?"

Maggie nodded. "You both will. Blikk wants you to alternate the role—you one night, Madelaine the next."

Excitement raced through me. So I'd finally get to dance the role I really wanted. Funny, I didn't even mind sharing it with Madelaine.

Mom and Daddy went off with Maggie. Luke tugged at Doug's arm. "This place is too jammed. Come on out of here and I'll show you how I won the Super-Duper Worldwide Easter Bunny Jumping Contest."

They left, towering Doug and stubby Luke. They reminded

me a little of my brother and willowy Madelaine. Just then she appeared out of the crowd. "Hi. Where's Luke?" she asked, glancing around.

"Off somewhere," I said, frowning at her pale, thin face and wondering how or if I should ask about her mother. "Uh, did you—did you find her, your mom?"

She nodded while her eyes shifted here and there. She must still be trying to locate my brother. And she was shivering even though she had buttoned her coat tightly over her practice clothes. Below it, her technique shoes were no longer immaculate but smudged and gray with dirt.

Questions about her mother kept crowding to my lips, but how could I ask them? Madelaine and I weren't exactly friends. Then, to my surprise, out of her mouth tumbled answers to the very questions I had wanted to ask but hadn't known how.

"We found her on a street corner. Not way off in the middle of the city, thank heavens. Only a few blocks from where we live. Sitting on a curb." Madelaine frowned down at her twisting hands. "Just sitting there. Sitting there and staring at the cars going by. At the buses. Breathing all that exhaust." Madelaine gazed past me as if I weren't there. She went on talking and talking. She couldn't seem to stop. "We got her into the car, Daddy and I, then to the hospital. They took her away. Two men in white coats. Orderlies, not doctors. Into the elevator, and the doors clanked shut."

Shuddering, Madelaine pressed her lips together. Tears shone in her eyes. Tears stung mine, too. My stomach tightened and turned over. And I had thought I had problems with my mom!

"It's good, isn't it, that your mother's in the hospital?" I asked. "I mean, they'll help her, won't they?"

Madelaine glanced back at me, blinking, as if finally remembering that I was there and who I was. Her cheeks reddened. "Sorry to be blabbing on and on like this. I don't know what got into me."

130

I could have told her, but didn't, that my mom, the psychologist, always says it helps if you can talk about your problems.

I only said, "Oh, that's okay," and examined a lock of my hair, anything not to see Madelaine's tight face and the tears spilling down it. My own face grew hot. "I'm really, really sorry about your mother. She's going to be okay, isn't she?"

Madelaine nodded. "Until next time. At the hospital they'll get her back on medication. It stops her thinking crazy thoughts. Doing crazy things. Hearing voices . . ." Madelaine's own voice drifted off.

I swallowed. "Voices? What's—what's wrong with your mom?"

Madelaine wove and rewove her fingers together. "She's mentally ill. Has what they call manic depression. Her brain doesn't work right. A chemical imbalance, the doctors say. You're born with it. It's in the genes, doctors think. Medicines help. If she'll take them."

"Hi, Maddy!" Luke said, speeding up to us. Stopping, he searched Madelaine's face. Maybe seeing the stiff whiteness there, he asked in a voice as deep as Daddy's, "Is everything under control?"

Her face relaxed and flowered into a smile. Would she ever smile at me like that? Could we maybe become friends?

"Hi, Luke. I've been looking for you," she said. "For the moment, things seem to be settling down. I've just been telling your sister all about it, haven't I, Cammy? More than you ever wanted to know," she added with a shaky giggle.

I hunched my shoulders. "I wish—I just wish I could do something to help, Madelaine," I said. And her smile and quiet glance told me that for the first time I had called the Paragon by her real name.

"Daddy dropped me off here just now and left," she said, turning to Luke again. "He had to go back to the hospital to sign some papers and things."

131

My brother nodded slowly, reminding me of a little old man. Then he sort of shook himself. "Bet you came to find out about the scholarships, didn't you? Well, good news, Maddy! You got one. 'Course you did!"

She smiled. "Claire told me. I met her on the stairs." And, with a glance at me, Madelaine added, "Half a scholarship, I understand. Which will be great because I really do want to be a dancer. It wasn't just Mama who wanted that. And you're getting the other half, aren't you, Cammy?" she asked, smiling at me.

I nodded.

"Yep!" Luke said. "That makes the two of you sort of Siamese twins."

Madelaine giggled. "Not twins. Our dancing's too different. Yours is so light, Cammy, so quick. Sort of like popcorn popping. I watch you and watch you and wonder how you do it."

My face grew warm. "You watch me? Really? But my *pirouettes* will never be as good as yours. Never as smooth and balanced."

Luke groaned. "All this lovey-dovey stuff! Think I'll puke! I liked it better before. Ever check out Maddy's extensions, Cameo Cammy? Miles higher than yours."

I grinned. "Yeah. I check them out every single day."

Madelaine laughed. "Just like I check out her beats and little jumps. We're good at different things, so there's room for both of us."

I nodded. "Maybe even room for creepy Luke," I said.

Luke tossed a bang of red hair off his forehead. "Is there ever! Room at the very top! That's what comes of being so terrific, plus being a boy. They add up to me. Lukenikov the Great!"